Breathing
Underwater

Breathing Underwater

Sarah Allen

FARRAR STRAUS GIROUX
NEW YORK

Farrar Straus Giroux Books for Young Readers
An imprint of Macmillan Publishing Group, LLC
120 Broadway, New York, NY 10271
mackids.com

Our books may be purchased in bulk for promotional, educational,
or business use. Please contact your local bookseller or the Macmillan
Corporate and Premium Sales Department at (800) 221-7945 ext. 5442 or
by email at MacmillanSpecialMarkets@macmillan.com.

Library of Congress Cataloging-in-Publication Data
Names: Allen, Sarah Elisabeth, author.
Title: Breathing underwater / Sarah Allen.
Description: First edition. | New York: Farrar Straus Giroux Books for Young
Readers, 2021. | Audience: Ages 10–14. | Audience: Grades 7–9. | Summary:
During a road trip, thirteen-year-old Olivia, a budding photographer, tries
to recreate a Treasure Hunt she once shared with her sixteen-year-old sister,
Ruth, while watching for signs that Ruth's depression is back.
Identifiers: LCCN 2020015760 | ISBN 9780374313258 (hardcover)
Subjects: CYAC: Sisters—Fiction. | Photography—Fiction. | Depression,
Mental—Fiction. | Treasure hunt (Game)—Fiction. |
Automobile travel—Fiction.
Classification: LCC PZ7.1.A4394 Bre 2021 | DDC [Fic]—dc23
LC record available at https://lccn.loc.gov/2020015760

First edition, 2021
Book design by Michelle Gengaro-Kokmen
Printed in the United States of America by LSC Communications,
Harrisonburg, Virginia

ISBN 978-0-374-31325-8 (hardcover)
1 3 5 7 9 10 8 6 4 2

To my road-tripping, pirate-diving, treasure-hunting sisters everywhere. I hope this brings you troves of happiness.

Breathing Underwater

CHAPTER ONE

Underwear: check.

Toothpaste and toothbrush: check.

Murphy, my stuffed killer whale, who Ruth has already made fun of me for packing: check.

I tried to keep him tucked under my clothes so Ruth wouldn't spot him if she came into my room. I didn't want her to see that I was bringing him and say, *Geez, Olivia, are you thirteen or three?* But she did come in, and she did see him, and she did say it, so I guess there's nothing I can do about *that*. That's just Ruth being Ruth, not one of the bad signs I need to watch out for.

Most important, I have my new underwater camera in its own special case, a purple case with a long black strap. It took me four months and extra chores to save up for this camera, but it was more than worth it.

I'm sitting cross-legged on my bedroom floor next to my mostly packed luggage when Ruth pokes her head through my doorway. As quickly as I can, I slide the four old pictures I'm looking at under my suitcase. This time Ruth doesn't notice. "Mom and Dad want us downstairs," she says.

"Mmkay, coming," I say. Ruth steps out of view. "Hey, Ruth?"

Her head pops back into frame. "What."

"Um . . ." Now I'm hesitant, but I say, "What do you remember most from last time?"

"Last time?"

"Yeah."

She shrugs. "I dunno. It was years ago."

Only three years ago, I think. "Do you remember what's in our secret box?"

"I dunno," she says again.

I nod. Ruth disappears from my doorway.

It's not like our secret box is huge or special or anything. It's just a box. A simple wooden box about the size for shoes. Ruth and I thought it looked like a treasure chest when we were younger, so we put a few of our most treasured things inside, like Polaroid pictures and key chains and plastic bracelets and shells we'd collected. We buried it in a cave at Sunset Cliffs, San Diego, before we moved away three years ago. Not even a cave, really, more an open room in the cliffs along the beach half a mile away from our old house. We walked there all the time, played there, and left our treasure there when I was ten and Ruth was thirteen.

And now? Now we're going back.

Only for a visit, true, but a visit where Ruth and I get to dig up our box of memories. Together.

There's another secret too. A secret plan I came up with as soon as this trip was scheduled. I haven't even told Ruth about it.

I slide the four pictures back out in front of me. Each one is from that first drive across the country, our big move. The first three are of Ruth: In one, she's jumping in front of a mural with the word NEW written on a banner across the top. The second photo shows her standing next to an old tyrannosaurus skeleton at a dinosaur museum, a matching tooth-baring grimace on her face. I remember we were both laughing so hard I could hardly take the picture. The third shot is more distant, showing Ruth on a bridge with railings covered in metal locks. She's got a hand on the railing and is looking out over the water, and she's wearing the green pants she used to wear when we played pirates.

When Ruth and I were little, we used to play pirates the way most people play the floor is lava, jumping around couch cushions on the floor, making each other walk the plank off the edge of the couch, battling with empty paper towel tubes. When we found small treasures we could keep, we used our special wooden box as the treasure chest.

The pictures make me grin even though I've seen them thousands of times before. I want to take them with me on the trip, but would rather not risk damaging them or Ruth seeing them. They might spoil my surprise.

The fourth and last picture is from the very end of that trip. It's of both of us, each with a moving box in our arms, standing in front of our new house for the first time. In the photo, the sunset makes the walls and windows glow. I wonder if Ruth would see what I see when I look at these pictures. Would she remember what she was thinking? Would she recognize the same story as me, or would it be different? Would she see happy leaps into the air and golden, glistening walls?

Mom's voice calls from downstairs. "Olivia!"

Mom, Dad, and Ruth are already seated at the

kitchen table when I come down. Ruth is in her big black hoodie. She wears hoodies even on hot summer days, and in Tennessee that is *something*. Usually she goes for black or dark blue, her favorite colors since forever. The colors of the deepest ocean, she says.

"How's packing?" Mom asks. She's got ridged worry lines at the corners of her eyes, but the most elegant smile and cheekbones. Her eyes are clear and smart, like she notices and understands everything, which fits with her job as a college professor.

"Basically done," I say. Ruth leans back in her chair, quiet, and lets my answer stand for both of us.

"Ellie and Eddie are going to be here at eight forty-five so you can load your stuff and be on the road by nine, okay?"

"Awesome!" I say.

Eddie is my mom's cousin. Her favorite cousin, who she's been close with basically her whole life, so he and Ellie have been more like an uncle and aunt to us. When they mentioned that they were renting an RV and taking a cross-country trip, my parents agreed to let Ruth and me go along. My parents both have to work this week, but they'll meet us at the end of the road in California.

Ruth stays quiet. She's not allowed to bring her

iPod to the table, but I swear most of the time it's like she's got music coming through invisible earbuds anyway. And yes, Ruth still uses an iPod. A big, old 80-gig one because she says it fits all her music, the battery lasts longer, and she never has to worry about losing service or taking up space on her phone.

Her iPod—her music—used to be part of our favorite game. Ruth came up with it when we were little, and the game grew and grew until it became what we called Treasure Hunt. Ruth would pick a word—*purple, heavy, flying, imaginary*. Then we would play as our favorite pirates. She would be Anne Bonny, I'd be Mary Read, and off we'd go to collect our treasure: purple treasure, or heavy treasure, or flying treasure, or imaginary treasure. I'd go off with my camera (the small point-and-shoot one I had back then), Ruth with her notebook and iPod. When we got back together, Ruth would have a music playlist written down and ready to go, filled with songs inspired by the specific treasure. Me? I'd have photographs. Then we'd listen to her playlist and I'd show her all my treasure photos. We did the purple Treasure Hunt at Mom's old university in California, and when we were back home, we listened to "Purple Rain" by Prince and I showed

Ruth pictures of a jacaranda tree with purple flowers, their petals flittering to the ground.

The best Treasure Hunt we ever did was the one Ruth planned for our big move three years ago. Four Treasure Hunt words spread across the country. Four words, with four perfect pictures, pictures that capture the music and smells and *feel* of that time, a happy time.

Now we're driving across the country again.

Hence, my secret plan.

"Ruth, you packed your medicine?" Mom asks.

"Yeah." Ruth absently reaches for the bowl of grapes in the middle of the table, and Dad scooches it toward her. His eyes blink, a little tired under his bushy eyebrows. Apparently when I was a baby, I used to try to catch those eyebrows in my hands like they were caterpillars.

"You know the Instagram rules," he says.

"Yep," I say. "No direct messaging and no pictures of my face."

Ruth looks at the table and stays silent. I catch both Mom and Dad glancing at her.

I'm pretty sure Ruth is excited about this trip like I am, and excited about finding our box again, even if she doesn't show it as much. That's what I think, anyway. Because who wouldn't be excited about a cross-country road trip in an RV? Digging up buried treasure? And pirate ships?

That's right, pirate ships.

Okay, so the ships at Wreck Alley aren't exactly *real* pirate ships; they were built to be sunk for the coral and scuba-diving tourists like us, with professional guides to keep us in the safe zones. Still, though. *Pirate ships*. And the ships are only about a mile or so off the beach from that cave at Sunset Cliffs, where our box is buried. After we get to the beach and dig up our treasure box, it will be like those Mary Read/Anne Bonny days all over again. But even more real this time.

And of course there's my plan for this trip. If I told Ruth outright that I've researched and strategized a reverse version of the Treasure Hunt we did on our first drive across the country, she might shoot it down or roll her eyes or just say she's too tired, but I've got something more stealthy in mind.

Ruth knows about our box, how we're going to dig it up together. But she doesn't know that the box is the treasure at the end of a cross-country Treasure Hunt, the way unboxing our stuff in our new house was last time. She doesn't know about my plan for secret pictures, secret replica images from our first trip, and when she sees them, she'll

understand. She'll see how much the good things—
our treasure—mean. She's got to.

Even though nobody has specifically said out
loud that this trip is for her, it is, a little bit. Her
doctor said getting out and experiencing new
adventures would probably be a good thing for
her. Plus connecting with past happy memories.
Memories of us playing loud music and jumping
around the couches wearing billowy T-shirts and
eye patches after counting our treasures. This trip
checks both those boxes perfectly.

"Okay," Mom says. She gives the okay sign. We
all tend to use that sign, the thumb and pointer
finger together making a circle, instead of the
thumbs-up. It's a leftover habit from learning some
signs when we were getting scuba certified. In
scuba-speak, a thumbs-up means *Heading to the surface right NOW, we need to end the dive!* Not exactly
the same as *okay.* Mom says, "I'm just going to go
over the calendar one more time."

Mom is super good at planning trips like this.
She's brilliant at seeing all the little puzzle pieces
and logistics and fitting it all together and taking
care of all the details. We're going over the plan
again, though, because she's also a worrier. I think
I get that from her.

Here's the plan:

Ruth and I will be driving from our home here in Knoxville to San Diego in Ellie and Eddie's RV. Mom's giving a lecture about women in the Tang dynasty at a summer conference at the university, Dad will present his graphic designs to a new client for their website, and then in about a week they will fly out and meet us in San Diego, where we will all visit familiar places and explore pirate ships.

And Ruth and I will find our secret box.

And I will reveal my secret pictures, our old and new memories.

And Ruth will have real treasure again.

I've tried to remember what we put in that box. I can remember most of it. At the time, my favorite possession was an old Polaroid camera, the kind of camera that printed out the pictures right as you took them, and you waved the photo in the air until the image appeared. Like magic. When I could get film, that's the camera I used on our Treasure Hunts. Pretty sure there's half a dozen Polaroids of a random smattering of purple things in that treasure box. I'm excited to compare those to my more recent photos to see how much my photographic composition skills have improved in the last few years.

I put in lots of other pictures too, some from the Polaroid, some printed from other cameras. Pictures of our boxer dog, Ramses. Pictures of Mom and Dad working at the kitchen table. Pictures of Ruth riding her bike, holding her old stuffed animal, listening to music, or wearing the baggy old white T-shirt she used to pretend was her pirate blouse. I remember those pictures. I remember her being happy in those pictures.

"You guys really going to be okay?" Mom says.

"You can call us every night," Dad says.

I spread my arms out wide at my sides. "It's gonna be incredible!"

I watch Ruth trace a finger across the wood grain of the table, and I wonder what's going on behind her tired eyes. I know there have got to be happy memories in there. The Ruth from those pictures is in there somewhere. My plan for the next week—my plan for this trip—will be to remind her. And tomorrow, the plan begins.

Tomorrow, we go on a Treasure Hunt.

CHAPTER TWO

Ellie and Eddie pull up in the RV at 8:37 a.m. Three minutes later, my bags are loaded up and I'm ready to go.

"Somebody's excited," Eddie says, grinning.

"Heck yes," I say, and we high-five. I know he's just as excited. One of our stops along the way is in Houston, where their daughter, Darcy, is going to college. It's one of the things that got the idea for this trip started, and we're all excited to see her again.

This trip developed slowly, like an emerging photograph in a darkroom, and it's finally about to be displayed in full color.

"Okay, guys," Ellie says. "I have researched

basically every best food stop between here and California, so get ready to eat!"

Ellie and Mom talk together for a minute, quietly. They've known each other so long that they share mannerisms, like the way they talk with their hands. I can't hear what they're saying, but Mom says something with a worried face and Ellie puts a hand on her shoulder. Ellie's good at that, knowing what other people need. She's the one who's always got extra hair ties, Neosporin, or hand sanitizer in her purse. And she introduced Ruth to the album *Love at First Sting* by the Scorpions.

I run my hand along a painted stripe on the side of the RV and give it a soft pat.

"Isn't she gorgeous?" Eddie says, coming up behind me. He looks up at the RV like it's a majestic elephant at the zoo. He's always looking at things and talking about things like they're utterly wonderful, and it makes it easier for me to look at them that way too. Like I have permission to see things effervescently. He's the one I picked when I needed to interview someone outside my immediate family for a school project.

"Most spectacular thing I've seen today," I say.

This giant RV is our home for the next little

while. Our home away from home until we reach the Pacific Ocean. All the way to relaxing on the beach, scuba diving at pirate ships, and digging up old, happy memories.

The digging-up part is just me and Ruth. A little bit like it used to be.

I sense something hiding under the waves of this trip, like the treasure itself. It's a trip on roads and through towns and cities, yes, but it's also a trip through those memories. Through who we were, which means who we still are, and who we can still be. The move years ago had been exciting for us, for the most part. I'd had a few friends I was going to miss, and leaving our house was scary, but new adventures were exciting, weren't they? Plus I'd still have Ruth, and that's what mattered. She'd started having a few dark moments before the move, but she told me she was excited about it too, that maybe after a move things would be better. We had so much fun doing the Treasure Hunt across the country I thought things were getting really good again. It wasn't until after the move that she started feeling . . . far away.

Mom and Dad sandwich me in a big hug.

"Be safe," Mom says. "And be good for Ellie and Eddie. Remember the Instagram rules. I'm so, so excited to see all the pictures you take."

"And have fun," Dad says.

Ruth steps out onto the front porch with her luggage, the blue tips of her spiky black hair flashing in the sunlight, and Dad catches her in a tight side hug and plants a kiss on the top of her head.

"Hey, Mom?" I say.

"Yeah, sweetie?"

I step away from Dad and Ruth, and Mom leans toward me. Before we leave, I feel like I need someone to know at least a tiny bit about what I'm going to try to do. "I've got kind of a surprise planned for Ruth at the end of this trip and I really hope she likes it."

I don't want to say too much more about it, and Mom doesn't ask. I knew she wouldn't. She just brushes her hand down my hair. "My patient, patient girl," she says. "You always take such good care of your sister."

That urgent voice deep in my mind says, *But not good enough.*

Well, that's about to change. This trip is going to be more than good. It's going to be the Viking hoard of Treasure Hunts.

I look between the RV and my sister, then back to my mom. There's blue sky and concern reflected in her eyes.

"I hope it helps," I say.

Above anyone else, I think, Mom knows what I mean. That I'm talking about my plan and this trip and the pirate ships and . . . well, everything. Anything. Mom pulls me into a gripping hug, her hand tense on my back.

"Me too," she says. "Me too."

Mom steps over and gives Ruth a hug and says something in her ear that I can't hear. Ruth sighs and nods.

Then Ruth steps past me toward the RV. "Okay then, let's go," she says.

Ellie and Eddie are already on board. Ruth climbs up and I'm the last one in, and I turn around on the top step and wave at my parents.

"Bye," Ruth calls from behind me. "Come on, Olivia, close the door."

I call goodbye one more time, then close the door. I watch through the window and Mom and Dad are standing there, arms around each other's shoulders. I remind myself it's only going to be a week until I see them again.

Besides, I have Ruth.

Now we're ready to go. Ellie and Eddie head to the front. Eddie puts his Nashville Predators cap on his round, bald head and cheers as he slides into the driver's seat. There's a small bedroom with a queen bed in the back of the RV that will be their territory on this trip. I climb up into the loft above the driver's seat, the spot I've claimed since I knew this trip was happening. Below me, on the driver's side, behind the seat, I see the small couch, a tiny counter and sink, and then the bathroom. Across from that is a little nook with a built-in sleeping space. That will be Ruth's space. There's a shelf in her nook too, on which she's already carefully laid her book and a spare pair of earbuds. She takes out a notebook and pen and jots something inside— probably the title of a song or some lyrics she wants to remember, or poetic lines of her own making. Then she adds the notebook to the shelf too.

I peek over my ledge and Ellie looks up at me and grins. She's got a round nose that wrinkles when she smiles, and clear blue eyes that always look like she's thinking about something far away. She's got a big atlas open on her lap. She likes having a physical map to look at and see where we are, even though Eddie's plotted our course in his phone.

"Are we all ready?" asks Eddie.

Yes! I think.

I really, really hope so.

My sister's bladder is the size of a pea. Or something, because we've only been on the road for a couple hours, but she's already been in the tiny RV bathroom for almost twenty minutes.

I'm starting to get worried. I always get nervous when she spends too much time cooped up like that. Alone. It's not usually a good sign.

Finally Ruth steps out of the tiny bathroom and the door claps shut behind her. She tosses her phone onto her bed like she's mad at it and then collapses onto the bed herself and pulls out her notebook and pen.

I've stayed curled up in my loft. I watch my sister from behind the cover of one of my *National Geographic* magazines. My stomach churns and clenches like it always does when Ruth is mad.

Mad, though, is sometimes better than the alternative. Mad at least means she's there inside, that she's feeling things and functioning okay, and that her medication is allowing her to process feelings, even feelings like anger or frustration. Without the medication, it becomes too much.

I know Ruth packed the medication she takes for her depression, because I checked when she wasn't looking. Not that I expected her to leave it behind, accidentally or on purpose. But you just can't be too careful.

One of the worst parts about depression is that it's not like an outside illness, where you can see the broken bone or the red swollen nose. It's an inside illness where you have to know the subtle signs.

Which is why I'm not super thrilled about her spending so much time alone in the bathroom.

I clutch my stuffed killer whale to me. I've learned to pay close attention to any of Ruth's signs that I *can* see because the last thing I want to be is clueless. If I don't pay attention, I might hurt Ruth in a way I don't mean to.

Maybe a distraction will help. "It is absolutely the most perfect summer day!" I call down.

"Shut up," Ruth says.

"Hey," Eddie calls from the driver's seat. "Let's everybody be nice."

Ruth grips the sleeve of her hoodie in one hand

and rolls her eyes. She plugs in her earbuds and twirls her finger around her iPod.

Even though it's the first day of what should be the most incredible trip ever, today is turning into one of Ruth's bad days. There are normal bad days, and then there are *really* bad days. The *really* bad days are when Ruth falls into what I call The Pit. I know the difference between a normal bad day and The Pit. I know the difference, because I know the signs. At least, some of the visible ones, I hope.

Sign number one: She's listening to John Williams. That's not so unusual, except that when Ruth is in The Pit, she feels words like barbed wire. She once told me that sometimes when people speak, it's like broken glass in her bloodstream. Which means that when she's in The Pit, even David Bowie and Freddie Mercury—her music gods—are out. She can't stand the words. So she listens to the *Saving Private Ryan* soundtrack.

Sign number two: She's wearing socks. Again, not so strange, except Ruth likes bare feet. Hood for her head, but nothing on her feet. Ruth's an enigma like that. This changes, of course, in The Pit. On the really bad days, her feet are so cold she could stick them straight in a fire and they'd still be frozen. I guess socks are the best she can do.

She hasn't told me this directly, but when she goes into her bedroom and emerges hours later with a deeper, hurting heaviness around her eyes and the quarter-note socks on her feet, I know.

Maybe socks and orchestral music aren't bad things, but they mean sad, hard things are happening in Ruth's head. Tender, painful things happening with her depression. Sometimes dangerous things. When her medicine isn't working like it should. When words start hurting. When she stops being able to sleep and no food tastes good.

The thing is, depression can look different for each person. And treatment can look different too. Before Ruth went to see the doctors, before she started taking medicine, it was like all her thoughts and emotions piled up in this swirling chaotic wave until it all became too much, tidal, crashing down into numbness. And it took lots of tries with different kinds of medicine and different doses before the doctors and Ruth found one that calmed the whirlpool going on in her mind. There were some that didn't really do much, or maybe even made it worse. Some gave her headaches when the dose was too high. Some seemed to work at first, but then it all came swirling back, along with extra nausea. But after experimenting, they found one that worked, and the right dosage to help Ruth think and feel a little bit more like her healthy self.

Ruth told me some of this herself—the tidal waves, the crash down to numbness. The rest is what I'm trying to learn from watching Ruth up close, trying my best to understand something she can only express in metaphor, trying to figure out what an inside hurt looks like on the outside.

I've tried to learn the signs. *Her* signs.

I want to watch Ruth's face when we find our old box and open it up and see the shells she put inside, and her favorite necklace, and the pictures I took of her. Pictures of us dancing and playing pirates and all the times when we were happy Treasure Hunters. Because I think that will be a good day. A really good one.

Pirates were the thing we always had in common, even when we had different taste in most other things, from clothes (I like stripes and polka dots, she likes black) to movies. I loved *Babe*, the pig movie, but Ruth said animal movies were dumb and the moving mouths were unrealistic anyway. I still love it, but of course I'm not going to say that.

Ruth's favorite movie is *Edward Scissorhands*. She says it has some of the best music *and* some of the best costumes. She made herself her own Edward Scissorhands suit for Halloween when she was thirteen, complete with carefully cut cardboard hand-blades. While a man with blades for fingers doesn't seem any more realistic to me than a talking pig, I'm not going to say that either.

We both love pretty much any movie about pirates. Even the cheesy ones.

My job on this trip is to watch out for the signs. That's *my* responsibility because I'm her sister. Ellie and Eddie know about things too, but I'm still the sister. That doesn't mean, though, that I can't take advantage of the situation. Because I mean, come on, pirate ships. Not every girl gets to go on a cross-country road trip in the loft of an RV, and I'm going to make the most of it. This is going to be one of the greatest trips of my entire life. I'm going to make sure of it.

My head is pressed against the window, where I can look at the lollipop sky and the passing trees and the tops of cars that look small from up here. I wish I could see it all at once, and never stop looking. I've got that whole stack of *National Geographic* magazines, but I'm so distracted by the looking and watching that I haven't needed them very much yet. Even the telephone poles look beautiful today, and I can't resist taking out my special camera and fiddling with apertures and shutter speeds and taking a few shots. If I set a wider aperture, more light gets in, which is good for inside the RV, where it's a little bit darker. Then I play around with shutter speeds: faster for clearer images, slower if I want blurry things in motion. With my camera in one hand, Murphy next to my other, and my stack of magazines behind me, I could stay in my loft forever.

I take out my phone and pull up Instagram, where I've only got one shot so far. A cool, low-angled picture of the front of the RV, with crazy clouds in the sky behind it. It took me a long time to convince Mom and Dad that I needed to start a travel photography account so I could keep pushing myself and my photography skills, so I could start growing my photography career, maybe even work my way toward getting some gigs, and that this trip was the *perfect* opportunity to start that up. Finally they agreed, with the caveat that I had to keep to the Instagram rules. Fine by me. I know I'm young to be a photographer, but Instagram means I can show people what this thirteen-year-old can really do with a camera in her hands. And I'm going to spend as much time practicing with this new camera as I can before we get to California and the pirate ships.

A feed of beautiful pictures, all helping me practice and get ready for one day being the best photographer *National Geographic*'s ever had.

There's a motorcyclist with a ponytail and a leather jacket in the lane to our left. I feel like banging on the window and shouting at him, *We're going to a pirate ship! We're going to a pirate ship!*

I slip a magazine from the top of my stack and flip it open. Even though I usually read every word (even the ads), today I just look at the pictures of luminescent pink jellyfish and fuzzy fur seals. The seals' eyes are reflective, and they're staring at the camera like it might be something good to eat.

If I had three wishes, I think I'd use all of them to be the person behind that camera.

I look down from my loft and watch Ruth's dark blue nails scroll through her iPod. Maybe I wouldn't use all three wishes on fur seals. I'd use the first one for something else.

When you're driving across the country playing Treasure Hunt, one word doesn't quite do it. You need several words, maybe even a whole rhyme. A rhyme Ruth made up, and one I've remembered for three years.

Something New
Something Old
Something Magic
Something Gold

These are the words I have sharpied on the back of those four pictures tucked carefully in my closet at home. I can see those four pictures as vividly as if they were in front of me again.

So really, my secret plan isn't *my* secret plan at all. It's Ruth's. But the idea of doing the same Treasure Hunt again as we go back across the country came into my mind like a gift. Because even though there were hard things about moving, we had each other. She's the one who sat by me every night while we moved away from everything familiar and played me music while we looked at my pictures. And Ruth doesn't even have to know I'm doing the Treasure Hunt, not at first, because I've got my camera. I can subtly take photos of Ruth at every stop, finding ways to replicate as perfectly as possible the images from the first time around. *Look at the pictures I took of you*, I'll tell her at the end. I'll surprise her with the pictures, and when she sees them, she'll know. And for the last and final picture—our Something Gold—we can have

Ellie or Eddie take a picture of us holding not moving boxes, but our Treasure Box.

We had each other then, and I want her to know that we still do.

Look at all the magic and gold treasures we've found, I'll say.

Olivia's Treasure Hunt Surprise. That thought makes me chuckle to myself.

Ruth planned the previous Treasure Hunt based on the major cities we were going to be passing through, dividing the clues among them. I've done the same, and was pretty excited when I realized that Something New would coincide with our first major stop: *New* Orleans. And now we're on our way.

I lean farther out from my loft, trying to get Ruth's attention. I try to think of something to say to her, a question to ask, just as an excuse to check in. Checking in is the only thing I can think to do to help. The only thing I've ever known to do. To make sure she's not getting sucked into her own little earbud world too badly.

I run my camera strap through my fingers and wonder what image could capture the time before it felt like our treasure was floating farther and farther away.

"Ruth," I say.

She pulls a knee up to her chest and ignores me, but I know she can hear me.

"Ruth," I say louder.

She yanks an earbud out of her ear. "Stop, Olivia. Yes, I'm fine. No, I don't care how many new followers you have on Instagram. Or whatever else it is you're going to ask me. Just leave me alone for two seconds." She puts the earbud back in and slides deeper into her bed.

I swallow and pull myself back into the loft. For the millionth time in my life, I feel a little crazy at all the things I can't do for my sister. I try—try to do something that will help—and half the time I just make things worse. As I watch her, I burst with the desire to pull down the sun and warm her feet. Or do *anything*. But I also know that sometimes just seeing the sun, or my face, makes her shadow darker. And so I sit, Buddha-like, while my stomach and heart do cartwheels around each other.

A Treasure Hunt that's both old and new will show her all the things I want her to see. *That's* something I can do.

That's what I love so much about a good photograph.

Ellie heard Ruth's frustration and is watching her

over her shoulder. After a moment, Ellie unclicks her seat belt and walks casually back to the mini-fridge by the couch. She pulls out two thermoses of water and two plums. She sets one of the waters at Ruth's feet and holds out a plum.

"I'm fine," Ruth says, looking at her music.

"Eat," Ellie says softly.

Without really looking, Ruth takes the plum and bites into it. Ellie leans back onto the couch and eats too. They don't talk, only eat while Ruth flips to the next song. As she gets some food in her, I can see Ruth's shoulders relax a bit.

Ellie is good at this. Natural, like she knows what to do without really having to try.

When Ruth's done eating, she holds her pit out and Ellie takes it and throws the pair of pits into the trash under the sink.

And like that, everything seems a bit more calm.

I watch my sister.

Something New. Something Old. Something Magic.

And at the end, Something Gold.

CHAPTER THREE

Pictures in or from a moving RV are a real challenge, even if you're *trying* to get a blurry motion shot. I want all kinds of pictures, blurry and otherwise, so for sure this is going to require some creativity and resourcefulness. I take a few test shots with my camera to make sure I know these settings like Ruth knows Billy Joel lyrics. I'm not going to get the most absolutely perfect shots, or even Instagram-worthy shots, if I can't maneuver across settings backward and forward without thinking. I need to know how F-stops connect to apertures and how pictures come out if the F-stop's set larger or smaller and what works best when it's lighter or darker and all of those professional photography things. It's got to be second nature.

"Why are you taking pictures of telephone poles?"

I turn around. Ruth has been watching me. I open my mouth to say something, but no words come. I shrug.

"You're so weird," she says, and puts her earbuds back in.

Ellie's got her atlas open across her lap and I can tell she's listening to us. She glances over her shoulder at Ruth. Then she looks up at me and catches me looking back.

"Hey," she says. "Do you know the alphabet game?"

"The one where you see who can find the alphabet first on, like, license plates and billboards and stuff?" I say.

"Yep. Bet you can't beat me."

"Oh, you're on," I say. "Ruth, we're gonna play the alphabet game."

"No thanks," Ruth says, flipping a page in her notebook.

I lean a little farther out from my loft. "You sure? It's fun."

She adjusts her earbuds. "Yeah, I'm good."

"But—"

"That's fine," Ellie interjects. She looks up at me

and winks. "If Ruth doesn't want to play, that's fine. It'll just be us two, and I'm still totally going to beat you. Eddie, you're our referee."

"Aye-aye, captain," he says.

Is it fine? Isn't Ruth missing out? But Ellie turns in her seat, looking out the windshield, then her side window. "*A . . . B!*"

I grin. The game's afoot! I hurry and flip myself over so I'm facing the front window, ready to scan for letters. Can't let Ellie get too much of a head start.

For the next little while, Ellie and I call out letters. We both get stuck on *V* for a long time until we spot a sign for a veterinary clinic. After I win the game at the last second (hooray for pizza billboards), Eddie takes an exit off the freeway and pulls into a QT gas station (could have used that one a few letters ago). I tuck a stray strand of hair behind my ear and climb down out of my loft. I think about bringing my camera, just in case, but lugging my camera into a gas station might make Ruth think I'm even weirder.

Instead I meander around the shelves. I halfway start looking for things I could take pictures of for New Treasure, but it's not quite time yet. Close, though. We're getting closer and closer to New

Orleans. I look at a spinning display of key chains. My favorite one says, *I'm not bossy, I'm just always right.*

Whether or not it's New Treasure time, my mind still settles back to photography. There's a sunburned man in a Stetson by the beer and a couple of girls with big, curly hair looking through magazines, and sometime I want to try one of those Portraits of Strangers projects I've seen. Projects where photographers go around interviewing random strangers, taking incredibly open and precise photos of someone they've barely met.

Ruth isn't really looking at the food, but wanders around looking at her phone. She stops and eye rolls at it.

"Friend drama?" I ask, risking the eye roll being redirected at me.

But Ruth holds up her phone. "Mom," she says. "She's already bugging me about making sure I take my meds and putting GIFs like that's going to make it less annoying. Also she's terrible at GIFs."

Of course Mom's worried. When Ruth started taking daily medication for her depression, my parents reacted kind of differently. My mom made a spreadsheet and set alarms on her phone and Ruth's, plus reminders twice a day that said *Time to hydrate!* Dad made a box shaped like a skull, the top half hinging upward like a doorway to the brain, and a slot inside perfectly shaped for a pill bottle. Mom groaned when he brought it out, but Ruth thought it was hilarious.

I don't tell Ruth I watched to make sure she took her pills that morning.

Not that she's in the habit of skipping or forgetting, but with a brain or a sister (or a sister's brain), you can't be too cautious. Instead I casually show Ruth where the granola bars are. The ones with the cherry filling. She's always liked cherry. Getting enough food is always a good thing, right? Not that food is something that automatically cures Ruth's bad days or anything like that, but it helped when Ellie did it. Ruth picks up one of the granola bars and after we pay at the register, she drops it into her purse. I hope she doesn't forget about it. Ruth losing her appetite is not a good sign.

That night we stop at a Waffle House for dinner. We're all fans of breakfast dinners, even Ruth. After we eat, Eddie gives me a couple quarters for the machines in the front lobby that spit out stickers or plastic rings or washable tattoos in little plastic carriers. I go for sparkly tattoos, because I'm pretty sure that's the one Ruth would go for.

My perfect Instagram shot hasn't happened today yet either. I try a few shots in the Waffle House parking lot on our way out, but nothing quite works. I don't get discouraged, though, because the sun is going down and even though night photography is super hard, it can be the coolest stuff when it works out well.

We park for the night, and I knew my hopes weren't in vain because across the street is a streetlamp and a giant oak tree.

Perfect.

Being out there alone with my camera and the nighttime breeze is my happy place. Happy in the peaceful sense. Happy in the sense that my head can finally stop buzzing about like a hyped-up bee.

I close my eyes for a few moments before I start shooting photos. It smells like cut grass and tar out here by the road. Sometimes I feel like smells can be important for getting my mind in the right place for a good picture.

I get a very atmospheric light-through-the-branches-type shot that will work just fine for a travel photo. I tend to go for the closer-up macro shots rather than the sweeping landscapes. That's becoming part of my signature style. The aesthetic I'm developing on this trip.

The screen door of the RV claps shut from behind me.

"There you are," Eddie says. "Everything okay?"

"Oh yeah, just getting a picture of the tree."

"Ooh," he says, grinning. "Can I see?"

I flip on the display screen and angle it toward him. He leans in, squinting.

"Wow, wow, wow." He puts his hands on his waist. "You have some serious talent. This is what you post on your Instagram?"

I nod.

"Wow," he says again. "This may be the thing that finally convinces me to sign up for social media. You've gotta show Ellie."

We climb up into the RV. Ellie and Ruth are both in PJs, flossing and brushing their teeth at the sink.

"Hey, El, look at the picture Olivia took."

My face is in danger of heating to a blush, and though I'm not really sure how to handle the attention, my skin buzzes with shy satisfaction as I turn my little camera screen toward Ellie. She stops flossing and leans in.

"Whoa," she says. "I love the angle here—that's

so cool! And the contrast . . . you're really good at this, Olivia. You should show us all the best pictures as we go . . . ooh, maybe at the end you could do some kind of, like, road-trip-recap slideshow too!"

"Definitely," Eddie says.

My laugh is awkward, but real. "Sure," I say.

Ruth's still brushing her teeth at the sink, looking in the mirror. Ellie heads to the back room, and Eddie steps up to the front of the RV to get his phone.

I pull the tattoo out of my pocket. It's a glittery silver-and-blue manta ray. I hold it out to Ruth, who spits toothpaste into the sink and looks over at me.

"I thought this was cool. I mean, I thought it was sort of *you*."

She tilts her head to look at it. "Cool. Thanks," she says, then scoops a drink of water in her hands. After she's rinsed and dried, she takes the tattoo square and sets it on her shelf.

I use the tiny bathroom to change into pajamas. Before I climb up into my loft, Eddie walks by and nudges me with his elbow.

"I think I've figured out what your superpower is," he says.

"My superpower?"

"Yeah, everyone has one. Yours is finding pretty

things to show other people. To try to make them happy."

Red lights of an ambulance rush by. "Ha, that's not a superpower," I say. "I wish it was."

"Believe me, it is," Eddie says. "Not everybody thinks that way, and you're really good at it."

If I was really good at making people happy, I think, then the people around me wouldn't be sad. But I tell Eddie thanks.

In my loft I upload the day's pictures onto my laptop. I sit cross-legged and spend a long time scrolling through the small moments of the day. Blurry trees, an aerial shot of Ruth with her earbuds in and eyes shut. (Not a New Treasure shot, but still a pretty good one.) That's what pictures are. Like a diary times three thousand.

The RV is dark except for the light from my computer. One of Ruth's legs is dangling off the side of her bed and her black-and-blue hair is mussed in every direction. A snore gets caught in her throat and she moans and rolls over. She looks so peaceful when she's asleep.

I get pretty in-the-zone when I'm going through pictures, especially now that I'm picking the very best ones to post. So it startles me a little when my phone buzzes.

Ruth: *You okay?*

I look down to her alcove and in the blue glow of her phone screen, I can see her looking at me. I must have woken her up. She looks back at her phone.

Me: *Yeah, just looking at pics.*
Ruth: *Weirdo.*

Then she sends a blurry, low-light photo of herself. The camera is just under her face and she's pressed her neck backward so it looks like she's got five chins. Her nostrils are flared and her teeth are settled on her upper lip in a ridiculous overbite.

I have to slap my hand over my mouth to keep from laughing and waking everyone else up. I don't care if Ruth gets mad at me tomorrow. That blurry picture will be a happy thought for a long time. It's the healthy, vivacious, laughing, pirate-ship, Treasure-Hunt-creating version of Ruth.

Me: *Your new profile pic.*
Ruth: *Get some sleep, you dork.*
Me: 😜

Before I shut down my laptop, I e-mail Ruth's selfie to myself. I download it and save it on my desktop in a new folder I name "Sisters." It's not a picture for my secret Treasure Hunt, but it's still a good one. Definitely a good one.

Then I close my laptop and put it in my bag. I find Murphy and lie down, pressing my forehead against the window. I scroll through the photos I've just uploaded to the cloud and find my favorite of the tree-streetlight shots.

One of the most boring parts about travel accounts, I've realized, is the captions. They're all so *Here we are at this gorgeous place blah blah blah.* I want to do something unique with my captions, give my photographs epic titles. I just haven't found the right idea. I look back down at Ruth and then it hits me. I know exactly what my caption strategy is going to be.

It won't even be hard. I already know all of Ruth's favorite songs.

And I remember a lot from our playlists.

In the caption space, I write: *"Moonage Daydream," David Bowie, 1972.*

Shared.

I don't even know if Ruth will see it. Maybe she'll think it's dumb. But I can't think of any other way to tell her what I want to say, to express it accurately. To tell her what I see. I don't know how to tell her that when I look back, I measure my life in Treasure Hunts.

So I'll do what I can to show her. Show her in pictures.

As I finally start drifting off, I imagine being the youngest photographer National Geographic has ever hired. I imagine professional travel photographers liking my work. I imagine them sending me a DM saying something like, *Hey, your work is great!* or *Hey, you've got a good eye!* or *Hey, you want to come photograph penguins in Antarctica with me?* And then being shocked when they realize I'm only thirteen.

I think about the Something New photo from last time, the one where Ruth's jumping high in the air under the sign, and I imagine how easy it's going to be to find something similar in New Orleans.

I imagine taking a picture that makes Ruth smile.

CHAPTER FOUR

Our Something Gold picture from last time—the one Mom took of Ruth and me holding our boxes, standing in front of our glowing new house—isn't quite the last Treasure Hunt photo I have. There's one more, from our last Treasure Hunt that we did only a few months after we moved. On my birthday.

We moved in the summer, and then in November I turned eleven. Ruth and I had only been in our new schools a few months. I was much too nervous to have a party that involved inviting kids in my class who I didn't know that well. So it was just the four of us: Mom, Dad, Ruth, and me.

The night before my birthday, Mom had tucked me in and told me she was sorry I wasn't going to be able to have a party with all my friends from back home, and I could tell she was worried. She didn't need to be though, because that zoo trip we did the next day became one of my favorite birthdays ever.

Ruth seemed tired, but when we walked through the gates, she grinned at me and said, "Geometric!" She pulled out her small flip notebook. I already had my camera.

At the zoo that day, sometimes we ran from exhibit to exhibit, and sometimes we sat for a long time and watched. Especially the gorillas. There was a new baby gorilla, and we watched it roll around and pull its mother's arm and chuck straw in her face.

I got a great shot of the shapes on a giraffe's neck. I took pictures of fish scales and polar bear noses and even the perfectly circular sewer cover. My best shot from that day, from that Geometric Treasure Hunt, was a close-up of the diamond-shaped scales on the crocodile's shoulder. Ruth jotted down song ideas and lyrics in her notebook. Sometimes her eyes got a little glazed and I had to remind her to keep going, but she didn't complain or grumble or snap at me or anything.

She didn't even get upset when, that night, I chose Boggle for our game. Ruth and I had already gone through my pictures and listened to her short "Geometric Treasure" playlist (with epic songs like "Turning Circles" by Judas Priest), and then we all sat up to the table. Mom had made a German chocolate cake, and we laid it in the middle of the table while we played and ate straight from the pan.

Halfway through round number five, I realized Ruth had put her pencil down and she was staring blankly at her paper. Mom noticed too.

"Hon?" she asked, so softly I barely heard. "If you want to go lie down, that's okay."

The words seemed to take a moment to get through Ruth's haze, but when they did, she blinked and shook her head. "No, it's okay. I can . . ."

She picked up her pencil, but her grip was so weak it dropped to the floor. She didn't even have the energy to bend down and pick it back up.

The sand in the Boggle timer ran down.

I put my pencil down too. "I know! Let's go watch *Edward Scissorhands*!"

Dad cleaned up the game and Mom got the movie set up. Ruth and I flopped next to each other on the couch. She'd been having some trouble sleeping, and I had a faint hope that she would doze off during the movie and get some rest, but my guess was that she probably wouldn't. She would stare at the screen the whole movie, like usual, so wide-eyed I wouldn't know if she was seeing every tiny thing that happened or seeing nothing at all.

I'd noticed Ruth's bad days for a while, even for a short time before the move. I'd started trying to learn the signs. But that was the first day I saw the real battle with herself deep in her eyes, in her shoulders and hands. That was the first night I saw how desperately hard she was trying.

I can't know what kind of effort it took, but as the movie started, Ruth nudged my side with her elbow. "Happy birthday, punk."

The RV smells of oranges when I wake up, and I can feel the rumble of the road underneath me. Through shut eyelids I register the brightness and I can hear the murmur of Ellie and Eddie's quiet conversation. There is a line of sweat along my sternum where I've clutched my stuffed killer whale all night.

A Journey song comes on the radio, so soft I can barely hear it, but I lie and listen and let myself keep my eyelids shut. I once heard a professional photographer on YouTube say that she spends some time every day with her eyes closed so she can keep her mental lens fresh. So I do that too.

And then I'm ready to find the perfect picture.

I roll away from the window and look out from my loft. Ruth is in her bed, with her iPod and a magazine.

We're going to be getting to New Orleans later today.

Something New, here we come.

Last time, our Something New day was in Las Cruces, New Mexico. We found murals that had recently been put up at Lions Park, with a big banner across the top that said, NEW INSTALLATION SPONSORED BY LAS CRUCES PARKS AND RECREATION. I pointed to the sign and said, "New! That's perfect!" Then I took pictures of Ruth jumping as high as she could right under the big green letters of NEW, her arms flung up high in the air. Throughout our day at the park, Ruth jotted down song ideas and built up a "Something New" playlist. That night we huddled on her motel room bed and listened to the songs—songs like "Brand New Key" and "New World Man"—and I showed her all my pictures, especially the jumping shots.

Later on, I printed out the best one. I wonder if she knows I still have it.

I don't think it's going to be hard at all to find cool new street art of some kind in New Orleans. Plus *New* is right in the city's name, so it probably won't even be hard to find somewhere for another jump shot of Ruth right under the word, just like before.

I roll onto my side and the loft creaks and Ellie looks up at me. "You awake, Olivia?" she says. She leans back and smiles. "How'd you sleep?"

"Great!"

"We got more oranges and yogurt," she says.

"Sweet!" I say. I hop onto the back of the couch and down onto the floor. Eddie turns the radio louder and I hum along.

I look up and realize Ruth has been watching me. "Great," she says. "Miss Perky's up." She rolls her eyes and goes back to her magazine. Oops. But Ruth's late-night obnoxious selfie is enough to keep me going all morning. Even if she's snippy now, that picture has to mean she's at least sort of okay. That the worst stuff isn't happening again. I'll keep on keeping tabs, of course.

Curled up on the little couch, I eat a quick breakfast, toss my yogurt carton away, then look out the window at the glorious day. The brush is thick on either side of us, but the land is flat and the sky is open and bright and cloudless. I watch out the window for a while, looking for picture inspiration, then climb back into my loft.

My phone battery is getting low. It's time for my turn with the car charger again. But I have a text from Mom that says *Call me.*

"It came," says Mom immediately.

"Oh, good!" *It* is a photography book I ordered that didn't come in time, a book with tips from real *National Geographic* photographers. "So you'll bring it to San Diego?"

"Yes! How's everything going so far? You guys okay?"

"We're all doing great. We're past Tuscaloosa now."

"Oh wow! And you guys slept in the RV last night?"

"Yep. It was cool. I miss you, though," I say.

"Oh, Olivia, I wish I could be there." She clears her throat, and I know what she's going to ask next. "How's Ruth?"

I knew she was going to ask that, and for maybe the first time I wonder about why. There are tiny questions beginning to whisper from opposite corners of my mind. Mom asks me how Ruth is doing because she knows I can handle the responsibility, right? That she can rely on me to keep the upbeat going. And that feels good, and feels like me. I *want* to be that person. But if that's a real, honest answer, then why do I also feel like I could truthfully say that I'm worried? How heavy a load on her shoulders would it be if I told her both answers? What would she do if I said I wanted her to know that yes, I, Olivia, am a happy person, but also, very frequently, anxious?

I glance down at Ruth. She's not curled into a ball. That's something. The tattoo square is still on her shelf, peeking out from under her notebook.

"She's okay," I say.

"Yeah," says Mom.

"Hey," I say. "Remember those murals in Las Cruces? When we were on the drive to Knoxville?"

"Murals?"

"At that park, remember?"

"Oh, right! You guys took, like, five hundred pictures. What were the . . ."

"They were murals of roadrunners," I say. "Dad kept saying *meep meep*."

Mom laughs. "Oh yeah! I remember."

I remember how every time Dad made that sound, Ruth laughed. One time she laughed until she snorted. When we took pictures, I remember her lifting her arms way up high in the air like she was flying.

I check again to make sure Ruth's earbuds are in and she can't hear me. "That move was . . . the drive was happy for . . . for all of us, right? I remember it being happy."

I hear Mom inhale. "I remember Ruth hoping it would be a good move. Hoping really hard. You helped her with that."

So much effort went into that Treasure Hunt, and I think Mom is right about Ruth. Signs of really bad days had recently started popping up like Bobbitt worms, and maybe Ruth was hoping that a move across the country would wipe them away from the start. We were both hoping.

We talk for a few more minutes, about Dad stressing out about his new client, like he always does. About when they're going to be flying out to meet us, about her lecture. She tells me she's keeping up-to-date on my "travelgram" and I tell her I know, because I've seen all her comments.

I try to imagine exactly what my mom is seeing as she's talking to me on the phone. Maybe the scratches on her desk? Dishes in the sink? That might be a cool photo project one day—take two relatives, show the different things they see, far away, nearby. I wonder if there's a chance they'd ever be seeing the same thing.

"Tell Ruth I love her," Mom says. "And tell Olivia I love her, too."

"Very funny, Mom," I say.

After I hang up, Ruth asks about making a pit stop, and I'm relieved that she's speaking, if only to ask to pee in a toilet that isn't moving. When we stop and all get out of the RV, Ruth doesn't immediately follow, which worries me, but as I get into the service station, I look back through the glass doors and see her stepping down out of the RV.

This service station is a fancy one. It's got a big lot spread with a handful of eighteen-wheelers and even a fountain out front. They have a whole row of vending machines with much more variety than earlier ones. They have a spinner full of postcards.

Ruth walks into the restroom and I grab a couple of fruit leathers. After I use the bathroom, I get my camera from the RV and look around the parking lot for potential Instagram pictures. The closer we get to New Orleans, the more excited I am about the Something New pictures I'm going to take.

The sun makes me squint. In front of the RV is an oil stain that's shimmering in rainbows. I pull my camera out of its sling and aim it at the spot.

The sun is way too bright for a perfect shot, but I play around with the settings and see if I can get the white balance to work. I take a couple practice shots, but they go between bleached-looking and muddy. I'm fiddling with the settings again when Ruth's reflection appears in the oil puddle. I hurry and click before she can move. One more for the "Sisters" folder.

"Why are you taking pictures of the asphalt?"

I open my mouth to tell her that there was a cool rainbow, that she had shimmering colors across her reflection, that I was just experimenting and practicing and I knew it wasn't going to be, like, the greatest photo ever or anything. But when I see her raised eyebrow and wrinkled nose, I don't know what to say, and she rolls her eyes and heads back to the RV.

Eddie walks out of the station with bananas and sunflower seeds. He comes over to where I am and looks at the puddle I'm looking at.

"Oh hey, that reflection's kind of cool," he says.

"Yeah? I mean, I was taking pictures, but it's weird . . ."

He tears open the corner of his sunflower-seed bag. "If you think it's cool enough to take pictures of, that's what matters, right?"

"Ruth thinks I'm weird." The words blurt out of me. I'm not sure exactly why I wanted to say it, but somehow saying those words out loud to Eddie feels like a relief. Like I'm unloading something I've been trying to carry by myself.

Eddie looks at me carefully. "One person's weird is another person's Vincent van Gogh, and where would we be without our Vincents?"

For a moment I wonder if he means I'm the Vincent or Ruth is, and then Eddie's eyes wrinkle into their usual grin and I realize he probably means both. I also realize I'm going to have that "Vincent" song by Don McLean stuck in my head now for the rest of the day. I wonder if Ruth has it on her iPod. I bet she does.

Eddie's looking up at the sky, his mind on a tangent. "That's what's so great about the Impressionists and the Postimpressionists," he mutters. "They're painting an experience, not just visual likeness."

I look up at the sky where Eddie's looking. I wonder what he's really seeing, and if photography can paint an experience too.

Eddie sighs, looks back at me, and smiles. "Hey," he says, "let's see how many sunflower seeds I can catch in my mouth at once."

He pours at least a third of the bag of seeds into his palm, then chucks them high into the air. He doesn't even look around first to see if anyone is watching. The seeds clatter down around us like hail and despite his wide-open and upturned mouth, he catches precisely zero.

We step into the RV together, laughing.

CHAPTER FIVE

I've never seen a city as colorful as New Orleans. I made a wish when we crossed the Louisiana border, like I did at the Alabama and Mississippi borders. I make the same wish every time, and the brightness of New Orleans almost feels like the universe working to make my wish come true. Neon signs flash in the shop windows. Orange buildings are window-draped with hanging green plants, and white carriages with red roofs pull families of tourists. We pass buildings painted yellow and blue, and cafés with pink banners flapping. We drive through a street of redbrick apartments and pear-colored palm bushes.

There are going to be lots of chances for Something New pictures here; we've driven past lots of murals already, and lots of spray-painted and chalked art along the walls and sides of buildings. Shouldn't be hard at all to find the name of the city sprayed in big, bold letters somewhere, right? A Something New sign just like last time, only New Orleans style. It doesn't even have to be the same kind of jumping picture, just a picture of Ruth standing under a new *New*, similar enough that when Ruth sees it, she'll remember.

And it's okay that Ruth's not making a new playlist, because I remember the songs, even if she doesn't have them downloaded.

The first thing we're doing (Ellie has had this planned for weeks) is going to Café du Monde for beignets. Not the *very* first thing, I guess, since before we do that, we have to fit the RV into its slot among hundreds of other RVs on the asphalt plateau by the river. The forest of motor homes is almost beautiful.

I take some pictures of it, of course. No good photos of street art here, though.

We walk to the edge of this mobile city and call an Uber. The driver is a bald man with a friendly gap between his front teeth. I have to pay attention to understand what he's saying, because his Louisiana drawl is so thick. He's trying to tell us about a better place for beignets, but it doesn't matter because Ellie is determined to get the specific Café du Monde experience.

And so we pull up to the café. The noise of the crowd erupts as we open the car doors, but we get out and the driver flashes his gap grin and drives off.

The café is a short pale building, but its main feature is a large green-and-white-striped awning jutting out like a circus tent. The awning is rimmed with glowing bulbs that make me think of vintage movie theaters. The air is thick with the kind of sugary, buttery smell you close your eyes for.

My camera is out and up almost instinctually. I take wide-frame shots of the whole café, then try zooming in close on the awning and the glowing yellow bulbs. The crowd outside is a rainbow of motion.

It's not new street art, but Café du Monde is still new for *us*, right? Something here could work, maybe. I'll keep my photographer's eye open.

I follow Ellie inside to what appears to be the back of the line. When we stop, she slides her hand into her husband's and they look at each other like they know each other so well they don't even have to try hard to know what the other is thinking.

For a quick moment, I wish Mom and Dad were here. They'd both love this place. Dad would have loved the art on the walls, the whole vibe. Mom would have loved the history.

We step forward in line and Ellie leans toward me. "Hey, show me the pictures you just took."

My camera is already out, and I click to the shots I took outside, of the awning and round light bulbs. I'm getting more used to showing her and Eddie my pictures without feeling so awkward about it.

"Oh my goodness, that's gorgeous!" she says. "I'm so glad you're documenting all this."

Eddie leans in too. "Hey, that's awesome! I love the cool shadows you got."

"Thanks," I say. There's still part of me that feels squirmy about getting their compliments, but honestly it feels really good to show them pictures I'm proud of.

We are surrounded by clattering and chattering and bursts of deep, full laughter. Eddie and Ellie read a plaque about the history of the café and bask in the glow of vintage bulbs and well-fed people. Ruth is on her phone, maybe checking her e-mail or Instagram.

I take a few deep breaths. Time for some interior

shots, and I could do with more practice with this camera to figure out how to do one of those cool dim-light motion-blur crowd shots that would be awesome in a place like this. But then I think to myself, that would be an obvious shot. Look for the not obvious. The unique. The mundane that's not really mundane at all.

The new.

The line moves forward faster than I expect, and soon we are at the counter by the arched windows. Ellie orders two big plates of beignets and we wriggle through the crowd toward the edge of the awning. Eddie sees a group of people getting ready to leave and pounces on the empty table.

We have to find an unused chair, but soon we are all seated. My back is against the gate, a perfect vantage point for crowd watching.

After a short wait, a girl brings two platters piled high with steaming brown beignets. They are hot enough to warm cold hands and piled so high with powdered sugar I don't know where to pick them up. It seems like we're all having the same hesitation, but in a moment we all—even Ruth—reach for the plates and take a pastry, causing powdered sugar to sprinkle over all of us like snow. Before I've taken my first bite, I've got a sprinkling of white on my collar and Eddie has to wipe sugar dust from his glasses.

We all take a bite of the perfectly shaped, perfectly fried beignets and I see Ellie close her eyes and smile like a kid.

"So worth it," she says.

Eddie leans toward me so I can hear. He gestures at Ellie. "That happy face is worth however many hours of driving," he says.

I look over at Ruth and catch her almost smiling, the angry furrow gone from her brow, and I think I know what Eddie's talking about. I'd fly to China for dumplings if it would get that smile.

Maybe beignets are a good sign. Maybe there really is such a thing as magic, only now we call it baking. Ruth's iPod is in her pocket and her hand is cupped under her chin, trying to catch powdered-sugar avalanches before they tumble into her lap. I hurry and wipe my fingers on my pants and aim my camera lens at Ruth and click while she's got a sticky hand raised in the air and is trying to lick sugar off the tip of her nose. I don't think she even notices. A perfect photo for the "Sisters" folder.

Ruth looks around and mumbles something about napkins. There are none.

All of us are dusted somewhere with sugar. Ruth is licking white off her fingertips and Ellie brushes crumbs off Eddie's chin. I wipe my palms on my jeans again and try to dust the sugar from the front of my shirt.

Maybe it's the sugar, but I have a weird idea. I wipe my hands clean the best I can and, while the others seem distracted by their own messy fingers, duck under the table with my camera.

"Whatcha doing down there?" Ellie asks.

So much for trying to be subtle.

"Nothing," I say. But it's too late. Ruth's face pops under the rim of the table, one eyebrow raised in annoyance.

"Get up," she says. "You're being embarrassing."

I'm about to zip up my camera bag and crawl back into my chair, but then I stop. I want this picture, even if it's weird. Maybe I can best capture my experience of this place from under the table, and if so, it's worth being a little strange. Photography is about looking at things from different angles, isn't it? I think about what Eddie said about Vincent van Gogh. It's already too late to stop Ruth from rolling her eyes at me, but maybe she'll see the picture on my Instagram and see what I was going for. See how fun this shot could be. Maybe.

So I clear my throat and hold tight to the leather strap of my camera bag. "I will in a second," I say.

Ruth groans and goes back to her beignet.

I match my camera's settings to the dim café light. Then I spin around, looking at all the shoes and feet jostling and tapping in the crowd around me.

Ruth's shoes are the closest to me. They're an old pair of black Converse, thrashed, a tear in one side, and they're dusted with a sprinkling of powdered sugar across the toes. It's a test of my camera's focus features, but I aim it at that sprinkling of powdered sugar. There are red sandals and blue tennis shoes and fifty other colors in the background, and the lights above reflect in the shine of the floor. The focus works, and I kind of love the framing.

Click.

The shoes are not new. The floor isn't, the place isn't, not really. But something going through my mind feels new and it takes me a moment to pin it down. Ruth got frustrated with me, snipped at me a little bit, and I did my own thing anyway. That? That's pretty new.

I look at the screen, at the picture I just took. It's

weird and I love it. *I* love it, outside of what anyone else might say or think. If nothing else, when
people scroll through the Café du Monde geotag
on Instagram, mine won't be at all what they're
expecting.

I'll call it *"Diamonds on the Soles of Her Shoes,"*
Paul Simon, 1986.

CHAPTER SIX

Ruth's iPod has become her comforter. This morning I saw her listening to the *Interstellar* soundtrack. Great soundtrack, but not a good sign.

I had hoped the beignets and colorful city would help, but maybe they didn't. Maybe that's a temporary magic. I wish I knew what *would* help. What she needs. What she's thinking. I'll keep an extra-careful eye on her today.

Besides, Ellie and Eddie are going out to lunch with some old friends, so it'll just be the two of us. And I have some ideas of what we can do.

While Ellie's changing, I climb down and try to nonchalantly sit on the very edge of Ruth's bed. She keeps looking at her iPod, but doesn't tell me to go away or anything.

"Hey, Ruth," I say.

She takes out her earbuds. She's gone from the *Interstellar* soundtrack to *Far from the Madding Crowd*.

"What if we went for a walk while Ellie and Eddie are gone?" I say.

She shrugs. That's a yes.

Maybe today isn't going to be so bad after all.

Ruth flinches and puts a hand on her stomach.

"Okay?" I ask.

"I'm fine. Just a stupid battle in my uterus right now."

I dash into the mini-bathroom, open the small drawer where the ibuprofen bottle is, and run back out with the bottle. My . . . well, battle, happened the week before we left, thank goodness.

I give the bottle to Ruth, then get a water bottle for her from the fridge. She doesn't take the water, and dry swallows two little red pills.

She does say thanks, or mumbles it, then goes back to her iPod. I leave the water bottle on her bed, wanting to remind her to drink, but she's already back in her music and I don't want to annoy her more or make things worse. Something feels very satisfying, though, about being able to physically give Ruth something helpful.

An Uber pulls up to take Ellie and Eddie to their lunch.

"You guys sure you're going to be okay?" Ellie asks.

"Yep!" I say.

Eddie hands me a couple of twenties. "There's those restaurants right outside the park when you get hungry," he says. "Stick together."

"We will," I say.

"We'll pick you up in a few hours when it's concert time!" Eddie says. He kind of jiggles his shoulders in a silly attempt at a dance move and I can't help but laugh. Ellie shakes her head, but smiles.

"There's a Triple D down that way." Ellie points. "They do corn-bread casserole and a shrimp gumbo that's apparently to die for."

They glance at Ruth and she nods a quick goodbye, then Ellie and Eddie step outside. I stand on the RV's steps and wave as they drive away. In the humidity, my skin feels oddly like I've just poured honey all over myself, and I'm sure my hair looks totally greasy even though I washed it this morning.

I step back inside. Ruth's hair looks perfect, as always. Heck, she rolls out of bed with it looking perfect. I guess that's the advantage of really short hair.

Now that Ellie and Eddie are gone, Ruth is up, ready, and has her bag hitched over her shoulder.

"Ready?" she says. "You wanted to go on a walk, right?"

"Oh, um. Yes." I try not to use exclamation points in my voice or get overexuberant and risk popping whatever bubble of goodness is happening. "We could go get some food. And I'll bring my camera in case we find good places for pictures."

I hope that sounds nonchalant.

"Yeah, maybe," she says absently.

"Your hair looks super cute today," I say.

She doesn't respond.

I swing my camera bag over my shoulder, slide my shoes on, and we're out.

We cross the asphalt jungle, pass all the RVs, and start passing shops and apartments. Ruth keeps walking. I see some fast food places, but Ruth doesn't stop.

It takes me one block to realize that Ruth knows where she's going. Without any discussion, I am following her somewhere. I have no choice because I'm supposed to stick with her. I don't ask, because I know that she will do what she wants no matter what I say. How nervous do I need to be about this? She keeps an eye on her phone's map and maintains our forward heading.

After several more blocks, I finally say, "Want to stop for food somewhere?"

"Let's keep going," she says.

I follow her farther and farther away from the RV park. I so badly want to ask her where we're headed, but she'll just tell me again to keep going. I'm starting to get scared.

But we're on a walk, technically. This could be my chance, and I still have my camera. That is something happy that my mind can hold fast to.

I follow Ruth but keep my eyes open for Something New photo ops. I look down side streets and around corners of buildings, and the search takes some of the edge off my nerves.

New Orleans doesn't disappoint. Down the far end of a street to our right I spot a wall with a giant pink NEW ORLEANS sprayed in bubble letters across the bricks.

Absolutely perfect.

"Hey," I say, nodding toward the sign. "Look, let's go take pictures."

My chance for a matching jumping shot, I think. Or at least something close.

Ruth is looking at the map on her phone.

"No, we're going straight," she says.

"We can come right back. I just want . . . that

big pink sign over there, see? It'll be quick, just a few pictures."

"No, we're going this way."

"Ruth, come on, it won't . . ."

"No."

The intersection is empty, and she crosses the street. Away from the sign.

I stand there for a second, alone on the curb, while Ruth walks away, a boiling bubble of frustration threatening to pop inside me. I want to scream her name. I want to grab her by the wrist and pull her to the perfect picture. But if I pulled her, she'd pull right back, and only break free of my grip even harder. If I screamed, she would scream right back, or possibly ignore me, and I don't know which would be worse.

Do I go to the sign on my own, without her, when she's the point of the picture in the first place? And if I did, would she just keep walking away?

What can I do but follow?

We pass a Walgreens and a bank, then a mattress store and a row of fast food places that all smell like onions. I don't want Ruth to roll her eyes at me for being dramatic, but I'm starting to get really nervous.

Maybe it's good I'm nervous, because otherwise the mad would take over. Those big New Orleans bubble letters could have been my one chance for the perfect Something New picture, and now we've missed it. We've *missed* it.

I find the voice in my head telling me that I'll have other chances, and it'll be okay. I try hard to hold to that thought because that's the one I want to believe, and Ruth will talk to me even less if I get mad at her. I focus on that positive voice, try to put a lid on the anger, and keep walking.

I see a cemetery ahead of us, and I wonder if that's where we're going. For some reason that makes me feel better. Short of the zombie apocalypse, I think cemeteries are pretty safe places to be, especially in the middle of the day. They're peaceful and full of history and good photo ops. There are trees there too, and benches.

We stop in front of a white clapboard building with another green awning. The neon sign in the window says INKY GIRL. Ruth swipes out of the map and starts scrolling through something on her phone.

"No," I say. "No way. I am not going in there."

"So don't go in," says Ruth.

"This is . . . you can't do this."

"Oh, please," she says.

"But . . . but you're not eighteen. It's not legal."

She gives me a raised eyebrow and I know she figured her way around that one weeks ago.

"Mom and Dad are going to kill you."

"I'll survive," she says. "And if you tell them or Ellie or Eddie, I'm not going to the cave with you."

What?

Not go find our treasure box?

My hands clench, and my shoulders feel tight with panic. How long has she planned this? I just keep thinking, *She can't do this, she can't do this.* Do I sacrifice our box and call Mom? That would only make Ruth hate me, and besides, what could Mom do? But if I *don't* call, that's only putting off the really difficult, painful conversation that will inevitably happen when they see whatever Ruth is about to do to herself. And what am I supposed to do while she's in there?

Ruth's found whatever she was looking for on her phone, and for a moment I imagine stealing it and running. She looks up at me, hesitating. For a moment I think I see a flash of guilt in her eyes, but she shrugs and says, "I'll text you when I'm done," and walks through the glass doors.

I stand there, blinking, trying to decide what

to do. I watch Ruth through the window and glass doors. After a moment at the counter, a girl with tiny pigtails and ink up both arms takes my sister around a wall to where I can't see her. This isn't something I want to watch anyway, and I turn around and start walking.

I feel my breathing quicken, which is not easy when the air you're breathing is completely saturated with moisture. But I can't help it, and the hairs on my neck start to bristle. My stupid, ridiculous, stubborn big sister. How could she do this to me?

I look around. I am alone in New Orleans.

A quick shot of adrenaline pumps from my sternum to my fingertips, but I try to shake it off. I can handle myself. I'll be all right. I could ignore what Ruth said and call Ellie and Eddie, but they can't really get here in time to do anything either. I can be smart and safe on my own. I just have to make it through today, make it through the Treasure Hunt and finding our box, until everything can be happy again.

A few blocks down the street is the cemetery, and beyond the fence, a stone bench. I will go there and wait, in sight of the road, in sight of the tattoo shop. I won't do anything stupid. I will be okay.

I walk a few blocks, trying to stay calm. I take a few steps into the street, crossing toward the cemetery entrance. There is a loud screeching, scraping sound and a wide black truck careens around the corner so fast and so sharp it's almost on two wheels. The mud-splattered fender avalanches toward me. I can't scream. I can't even swallow. The horn honks and it's so near I can almost feel the sound waves.

I am going to die.

Some instinct kicks in and I roll onto the grass on the other side of the street just as the truck screeches past. My left arm scrapes against the gritty sidewalk. I lift my head in time to see the muddy truck tear around another corner. For a few more seconds I can still hear it, and it takes some time to understand that the truck is gone without my body splattered across it like an insect carcass.

For a second everything comes in gulps—my breath, vision, heartbeat. The injustice of my situation fills me up and threatens to spill out my eyeballs. I'm ditched, alone, in a who-knows-where part of a magical but strange city, and I nearly got turned into truck-paste.

A new worry pops between my eyeballs like a slung stone. "My camera," I manage to squeak.

I look around, and I see the camera bag behind

me. I pull the strap toward me, pretty sure that I actually *will* die if anything is wrong with my camera.

There's a small scratch across the front of the case, but the heavy-duty bag did its job. The bag somehow got flung off my shoulder and landed on the grass and my camera is still flawless.

I have my camera. I can take my travel photos and Treasure Hunt photos. Something New hasn't gone quite like I planned so far, but I can figure something out. I have my camera. I will be fine.

Eventually my breathing begins to calm down. I start to stand up, but my knees are so jittery I sit down again. My arm from my left shoulder down to my elbow is scraped and gritty. I feel the pain beginning to seep in, dull like a slow squeeze, but at the moment it doesn't hurt too bad.

Now that my panic and adrenaline levels are starting to normalize, I go over my situation again. My heart is still fluttering, but my thoughts are slowly coming back to me, and I shake my hands at my sides like I can shake my brain back into focus. It also helps hold back the wet heat starting to sting my eyes. If Ruth hadn't abandoned me, I wouldn't be sitting here, scraped up, by the side of an unknown road. I slap the concrete under me—how dare she leave me like this—but it only adds a hurt palm to my injuries.

In and out, I tell my lungs. In and out. I've got some scrapes, but I'm not seriously hurt. And Ruth . . . There are plenty of worse things she could be doing to herself. I sit there for a moment, just breathing, trying to remind myself of that. But Mom . . . Mom is going to feel hurt like *she* was the one getting jabbed with needles. It's the deception and sneaking that's really going to sting. Even from across the country I know how Mom's face will look. Dad will have the iron jaw, but Mom will look at her hands like they've failed her, like they've been bitten. How can Ruth not understand that?

And I will know even less what to do except watch Ruth more closely and stay right by my mom, trying my best, as always, to keep the upbeat.

So I pick up my camera and hold it to my chest because that is something I know how to do. I'm right next to the cemetery gates and now that my legs are starting to work again, I stand and walk through into the wet, wet green, and the garden of aboveground vaults of white stone. Many of the graves come higher than my head and I start snapping pictures. Pictures of graves shaped like pyramids, and one covered over with stone-carved angel's wings.

Behind the lens I lose my fear and all sense of time. I take a picture of the grave of someone named Ruth Pendergast, who's got *Sassy and classy to the end* written across the front of her vault. I think my sister will like that one.

I keep walking deeper into the cemetery. The part of me wishing my mom and dad were here right now is still pulsing loudly over my whole body. Maybe I can text them. I could find the funniest name here and send it to Dad, and the oldest grave and text a picture to Mom.

Under one of the trees I find a sleek black crow's feather. It's long, all its bristles in perfect shape, and it glints in the sun, even more metallic than Ruth's hair. With a blue tip it would pretty well match Ruth's hair, actually. I scoop it up and set it carefully in my camera bag.

My meandering leads me toward a gigantic knobby oak with long, mossy, bony-looking limbs coming off in all directions. It's seriously like something out of *The Twilight Zone*. There is sap oozing through cracks in the bark and I see a trail of ants crawling up through the tree like a maze. The ground has flattened out some, or at least it looks that way, since in this small corner of the cemetery, the graves are underground.

Through my viewfinder I see, on the other side of the tree, an old lady with white hair in a bun kneeling over one of these underground graves. She's clucking her tongue and wiping her hand across one of the stones, and her hand comes up wet and muddy. It's hard to tell from this distance, but I can just make out the layer of water covering the stone and I realize why most of the cemetery is aboveground. I think the water levels in New Orleans are high enough that it makes digging graves a problem. I think the ground here is just that wet.

Something about the old woman seems familiar. The angle of her chin, the slope of her forehead or maybe it's her narrow shoulders that make me think of someone I can't quite name. I look through my camera again and zoom in on her face. Her look of concentration. That's when it comes to me. Maybe I've got Ruth on the brain (like usual), but it's my sister the old woman reminds me of, like these are the lines that will be on Ruth's face when she's old. Through my lens I watch how carefully she tends the grave, and I wonder whose it is. Her husband's? Her mother's?

Her sister's?

I zoom out slightly to catch the woman on her knees, hand across the stone like a benediction, a jagged tree-branch shadow cutting across her face, and I click. Maybe she wouldn't want me taking pictures. Maybe there are rules about that kind of thing. I don't know, and in that moment I don't care.

"Echoes," Pink Floyd, 1971.

CHAPTER SEVEN

I photo shoot my way back to the entrance of the cemetery. I exit the cemetery, passing under the stone arch and back onto the street. I'm thinking about later that night when I will download all these pictures onto my laptop and post my favorite of the white-haired lady. Lyrics and captions run through my head.

A few blocks away I see the green awning of the tattoo shop. It's a reminder that hits me like ice water.

"Oh crap."

I slip my phone from my back pocket. I have three missed calls and a message. All from Ruth. I hit CALLBACK and start pacing.

She answers after one ring. "Why aren't you answering your phone?"

At least she's okay.

"I'm sorry, I was . . . distracted."

How could I have gotten distracted?

"What if you'd been abducted?" she says.

"Like by aliens?"

"Olivia! You know what I mean."

In my frustrated distraction I'm about to step onto the street but remember the truck and stop. "Hey," I say into my phone. "You're the one who ditched me."

"I did not ditch you," she says. "And I would have at least answered my phone."

My breath is coming out in angry spurts. I'm so used to shoving a lid on the angry pot until the boiling stops, anything to avoid spilling over and making Ruth feel any worse. But I want to tell her how unfair she's being. She did so ditch me. She's free to go get a tattoo, but I can't take a walk without her yelling at me?

"Where are you?" she says.

Then in the distance, I see Ruth emerge from the tattoo parlor, pacing back and forth with her phone up to her ear. She doesn't see me.

"I . . ." I hesitate. I suddenly don't want to tell her where I've been. Photographing the cemetery feels like mine. Like a Treasure Hunt I came up with all on my own, that I'll be ready to share only at the right time. Maybe I'll be ready to tell her more when I give her the crow's feather later tonight. I step back into the cemetery, behind the arch and gateway. "I'm just a couple blocks away."

"Ellie called," Ruth says. "I told her we're at the cemetery and they're coming to pick us up."

I sigh. "Fine."

"Meet me there right now."

"They're going to be upset," I say, thinking of whatever she's just inked on herself.

"Just freaking get there, okay?"

"Okay, okay."

I hang up. It feels unsatisfying, and for a second I wish I had one of those old flip phones so I could at least have hung up with a snap.

She was worried about me. She was a brat about it, but at least she was concerned. That's something. But she shouldn't be able to talk to me like that, should she? So much of it feels unfair. Anything I might say back would just make things worse.

A couple of blackbirds land in the tree above my

head. I stand at the cemetery entrance, waiting for Ruth.

We all got scuba certified the summer I was ten, right before Mom got offered a job at the University of Tennessee and we learned we were leaving California. Despite weeks of lessons and practice dives in the training pool, we never got the chance to go diving at Wreck Alley before we moved away from the ocean.

The lessons were toward the end of the school year, right at the beginning of summer. Those weeks were the beginning of Ruth's really bad days. When I look back, that's when I think the depression first started showing itself, though she wasn't officially diagnosed until a short while after our move. That was the summer I first started noticing The Pit.

Even with everything happening, getting certified was still amazing. And it was something we all did together, Mom, Dad, Ruth, and I. Ruth was thirteen and we hadn't been playing Treasure Hunt pirates as much lately, maybe because she was focused on friends, maybe because she'd recently started having more bad days, or maybe simply because she was getting older. Whatever it was, I was excited to be back in the water with her, in a sense. Plus, Ruth decided she and I were going to teach ourselves a few extra signs, not just the scuba ones, including memorizing the alphabet in sign language. She'd look up tutorials on YouTube and we'd watch them and practice together. Sometimes in our practice dives in the training pool, I'd sign H-I R-U-T-H while we were underwater, and she'd sign H-I back.

Our scuba instructor's name was Anne Reed. If Ruth noticed the piratey name, she didn't say anything. I didn't say anything to her about it either, because I was trying to learn how to be watchful. I was trying to understand this trench-deep hurt my sister sometimes had and trying to learn what I could do to help. I'd learned at that point that on her bad days, my being overexuberant was *not* helpful.

I meandered over to Ruth's side of the pool, but stayed far enough away that she wouldn't think I was following her. She'd been distracted and a bit snippy that morning, but she was swimming and participating, so it wasn't the worst kind of day. She was wearing a white-and-red wet suit. Mine was blue and brown.

The indoor training pool went down to twenty-five feet. There were steps that went down and down under the water until the last big drop-off. I hooked everything up like I'd been taught, and slipped on my mask and regulator. I waded farther in, trying not to trip over my fins. I hated using them, but I did anyway, because Ruth did.

The pool was well-lit, and there were designs carved into the walls and the floor below. One of my favorite things was to go down to the deepest end and trace the designs on the bottom. I imagined taking pictures of the designs and tried to think of what Treasure Hunt words I would use those pictures for. I couldn't think of very many; that wasn't my strong suit. Having Ruth give me the words always sparked some new ideas I wouldn't have thought of otherwise.

The hard part of diving for me was what the teacher called a "buoyancy compensator"—the part of the gear that helped you sink lower or float higher. I wasn't as smooth with it as I wanted to be, but soon enough I was belly down on the pool floor, crawling deeper and deeper. I loved the way the blue-green light swam in the water. If I turned my head, I could see people swimming above me; I could see Ruth's black fins with the red stripe down the middle. What word would Ruth give for a picture like that, I wondered.

Soon I was in the deep end, around the drain grate. Along the edge were carvings of sea turtles and stingrays. I swam up close, my goggles inches from the concrete, and wished I had an underwater camera with me.

To this day I don't know what happened. In a split second, one side of my goggles had filled up with water and the other was full enough I had to close my eyes. It happened so fast it shocked me, and I twisted and flinched and lost my orientation. It took all my self-control not to completely panic and lose my regulator.

The water seemed to swamp my brain and I couldn't think. My feet were flailing inside their flippers. What was it I was supposed to do? I tried to remember. Something about floating to the top, maybe? Inflating something? I needed someone to remind me what I was supposed to do. I was sure I was going to lose my oxygen and start gulping pool water.

I probably would have been able to manage, would have thought of something, but before I'd had a chance to calm down, I felt a grip on the back of my arm. A firm grip, pulling me upward. I knew who it was by the feel of her hands.

When we broke the surface, I yanked my goggles off and pulled the regulator out of my mouth. Even though I hadn't lost my oxygen, it was still difficult to catch my breath, and I bobbed in the water, breathing hard and rubbing my eyes until I could see again.

When I'd blinked the last of the water out of my eyes, Ruth was there floating in front of me, goggles off, hair slicked back.

"I'm okay," I said. "I can do this."

For a second she just looked at me. In that flashing moment I could see the aching, sorrowful whirlpool behind her eyes, like a reflection in the water.

"Don't freak out next time, okay?" she said. Then she turned and swam away, back toward the deep end, pulling on her goggles and regulator as she went.

Our Uber pulls up to the concert hall and I hand Ellie back the Neosporin.

"You tripped going into the cemetery?" Ellie asks.

"Yeah," I say.

When they picked us up, Ruth told Ellie we just went for a walk. I stayed quiet.

Ellie says, "I know I already said this at dinner, but, guys, please don't wander so far next time, especially without telling us."

"I know," I say. "I'm sorry."

Ruth doesn't say anything. Neither Ellie nor Eddie has seen the small bass clef that's now behind Ruth's right ear. I saw it at the restaurant when I went with Ruth to the bathroom and she peeled the bandage back a little to check it in the mirror. The skin is red and swollen, but she's kept the bandage over it and kept her hood up and has so far managed to hide it from them.

We step into the lobby and there's a gorgeous glass chandelier sparkling above us. Eddie gets our tickets and we go into the auditorium and slide down the row to our seats. I land in the seat on Ruth's right, her tattoo facing me instead of Ellie and Eddie, and I think she finagled that on purpose.

Then the lights go down, and Ruth leans forward. The seats are soft velvet, and the audience around us hushes.

A blast from a chorus of saxophones shakes us in our seats, and bright white lights flash all around us before sparkling and closing in on the musicians up onstage. The pianist starts a rhythmic trill on the keyboard, following the drums' pulsing beat.

Neither Ruth nor I know much about this jazz group, but Ellie and Eddie have been excited about them for a long time. My sister's wide eyes reflect the stage lights, and she's smiling without thinking much about it. I think something about live music, whatever kind it is, fits inside Ruth's heart-space the way being behind a camera does for me. She seems open and free the whole show.

At intermission, Ruth turns to Ellie. "How did you find out about these guys? They're awesome!"

"Right?" Ellie says. "It was so random, actually. I was planning this 1920s-themed event for work and found them on YouTube and got totally obsessed. With New Orleans–style jazz generally and these guys in particular. I mean, the group improv skills . . . it's mind-blowing."

They start chatting about music, how Eddie played the trombone in high school and college. That's something I didn't know about him, and I didn't think Ruth would be that into jazz.

But I'm not paying too much attention to exactly what they're saying because there's something I don't get. After walking through a strange new city, after arguing on the phone with me, after getting an illegal tattoo that is going to get her in epic trouble at some point or another, Ruth's here chatting and relaxing in these red theater seats, enjoying a concert like nothing's happened. The tattoo—the incriminating evidence—is one wrong head-turn away from being spotted, but that doesn't seem to bother her at all.

After a few minutes Ruth goes back to poring over her program. On the open page is a picture of the musicians and the words *New Orleans Jazz Company*. I take out my camera, and as quickly as I can, take a picture of her hands holding the program, her thumbs pointing up toward the *New*. I try to make it seem like I'm just scrolling through old photos for a second, and she doesn't notice I'm taking a picture. I stash my camera again just as quickly, before any of the ushers notice.

This concert-program photo will have to technically count for my Something New picture, since tomorrow we're leaving for a new city and a new plan. It's a major stretch, and not at all the same kind of happy jump shot as last time. I'm not thrilled, but I did the best I could.

Then Ruth turns to me, looking exhilarated. "These guys are so insanely talented, aren't they?"

The lights shut off suddenly, then a spotlight illuminates a single trumpeter in the middle of the stage. He stands there, alone in the light, brings the gleaming trumpet up to his lips, and begins a high, soaring solo that reaches to the back of the audience, up to the tall, tall roof, and out into the black night sky.

A full moon spotlights me through the front RV window that night. I've drawn back the curtains in my little loft and stare at the moon, trying to make out a pattern in the dark smudges across its glowing surface. People say it looks like a man or a rabbit, but I can't see anything. Maybe it's too bright.

I hear Ruth breathing. She has this not-quite-snore that's more like choking in air and then puffing it out all at once. Some nights it sounds desperate and makes me sad, but tonight it is comforting. I've never been someone who likes sleepovers or too-long school trips or staying places at night without my family. It doesn't count as away from family if Ruth is here.

Despite all the things I don't understand, despite the tattoo, almost getting mashed by a truck, and not getting the picture I wanted, I don't feel home-sick when I hear her snoring. If only my plan for the Treasure Hunt would have worked out better. If only we could have walked back to that street art, gotten that perfect replica photo. I could see that perfect shot in my mind, those big letters, Ruth's shadow behind her on the wall as she jumped. If only Ruth would have stopped, just for a second, and let me take her picture. If only she'd listened to me once. If only . . .

The *if only's* are beginning to steam like a kettle on a hot stove.

I sit up. It's going to be hard to fall asleep tonight.

And I need to cool down before the bubbles boil over.

I climb from my loft onto the arm of the couch, making as little sound as possible. Even so, Ruth coughs and shifts onto her side. I pause, waiting until she's back to her normal breathing before I step down onto the floor. The RV door squeaks, and I flinch and pause again before I open it the rest of the way and hurry out onto the steps.

Warm nights are like being underwater, all-encompassing and new no matter how many times you've been there before. I let the night wash over me, pull me in and out like a tide. This kind of heat is way better than behind-the-eyes heat.

The door claps shut from behind me. I turn and see Eddie. He flinches from the noise.

"Oops," he says.

"Did I wake you up? I'm sorry."

"Naw, couldn't sleep either." He comes and sits next to me on the concrete ledge around the lot. He lets out a sigh and for a moment we sit in silence and watch wispy clouds pass across the moon.

"Your dad was texting me today, asking about you guys," Eddie says. "He's very proud of you, in case you weren't aware. He's always telling me about how well you're doing in school, all the travel books you're reading."

"And getting in trouble because I get caught reading during choir."

He laughs. "He didn't tell me about that one."

"He didn't? Yeah, I almost got sent to the principal."

"We're all human," he says, and winks.

An ambulance passes by, somewhere far behind us.

"Thanks for taking us on this trip," I say. "I think seeing pirate ships will be the most exciting thing I've ever done."

"Besides marrying Ellie and being a dad," he says, "me too."

Ellie and Eddie's daughter, Darcy, is our next stop. She's going to show her parents around the University of Houston campus, and I know how much they've been looking forward to seeing her again. I'm excited to see her too. She once came and stayed with Ruth and me when all our parents were out of town for a couple of nights, and gave us both manicures and pedicures. It's been a while since we've seen her.

Houston is also where I've planned the Something Old portion of our trip. I did my research, and Houston has a great dinosaur museum.

"It'll be fun to see Darcy again," I say.

"Oh man, yes," Eddie says. "Seeing her and Ellie together . . . I could be content just watching that for the rest of my life."

I'm not used to being talked to this way, without any hint of condescension or aloofness, the way most adults talk to kids my age. But Eddie is easy to talk to. He never makes me feel my own awkwardness.

"It's really great when they're happy," I say softly. I glance back at the RV. I think he knows what I mean.

"The best," he says.

"That concert was really cool tonight," I say. "I think everyone really liked it."

"Those guys are something, aren't they?"

A light breeze blows past, and frogs are performing a symphony out there in the trees. The music really was amazing, and Ruth soaked it all in. For a little while, she was enthusiastic and everything was okay. I want so badly to hear what's going on in Ruth's head. It's like there's some song in there I just can't hear.

I wish it was possible to take a picture of somebody else's thoughts.

"Eddie?" I say.

"Hmm?" His eyes are closed, his voice tired.

"Remember that thing you said about, like, one person's Vincent van Gogh and all that?"

"Sure."

"So . . . why? How come it's like that? Why aren't we all seeing the same thing? And if we're all seeing things differently, how do you know what people think or . . . or feel, when you can't see what each other is seeing? When you don't think you can understand at all even when you try?"

He opens his eyes and turns to me.

"Explain what you mean," he says.

Maybe I shouldn't have asked. "Well," I say, choosing my words carefully. "I mean, we're all different, right? We're all . . . seeing things differently even when we're seeing the same thing." I inhale the wet air. "So . . . how do you? How do you see the same thing?"

"Let me think," he says. He takes his time, like he's really considering my question. I wish all questions could be asked at two in the morning under a full moon where there was all the time in the world.

"It's hard to understand someone when they don't understand you. But trying, whether or not they understand you . . . well, to me, I think that's love. And I think that's what matters."

"Doesn't loving them mean you understand them?"

Eddie laughs and his shoulders shake. "Oh, I wish. Sometimes I look at Ellie and I think, what in the world is going on in that head? But I can't—don't want to change her. And she couldn't change me even when she wants to! The point is to love all of each other, all the different parts just as they are, even the things we don't get."

I twirl a finger in the hem of my pajama pants. "So how do you do that?"

He turns to me, the craning of his neck forming

a double chin, and he winks. "That's the kind of question you'll ask yourself over and over again for the rest of your life, and how wonderful is that?"

I think about Eddie's words for a long time, before we head inside. I'll be thinking about them for a while longer too.

When we do step back inside the RV, Eddie whispers good night and heads to the room where Ellie is sleeping. Ruth didn't move when we came in and both Eddie and I thought she was asleep, but after Eddie closes the back-room door, I glance over and her eyes are open. She's watching me. Feeling the colors of the city and the sound of frogs and the whispering breeze inside me, I sit on the edge of her bed. She untucks an arm and lays it across the top of her blanket.

A big part of me wants to tell her everything, tell her about this Treasure Hunt I'm trying to do. Ask her if she remembers all the details of last time, the way I do. Ask her if all those times, all those songs and pictures and words, meant the same thing to her as they did to me.

Instead I whisper, "Do you remember any of the pictures we put in the box?"

She nods, her eyes blinking with sleep. "Mm-hmm, some of them. Especially that one, I think you're in the bathroom, and I stole Mom's eyeliner to draw a goatee on you."

I try to keep my laughter quiet. "I remember that."

"Oh man, I remember we accidentally spilled eye shadow all over the sink." Ruth looks over at the couch and snorts. "Mom grounded us for a week."

"Yeah, she did. And then bought us face paint."

"Who were you trying to be again?" she says.

"Calico Jack."

"That's right. We went back to Anne Bonny and Mary Read after that."

"I'm excited to find that picture," I say, trying to gauge her facial expression in the dark. "I remember there's also one of you in your pirate blouse."

"There is?" she says, and yawns.

The tiniest, faintest voice has occasionally whispered in my mind that there's some chance our box *might* not be there after all these years, but I refuse to believe the universe would do that to me—to us. And most important, Ruth's never said it. So I won't either, even to myself.

The program from the concert is now on Ruth's shelf, along with the crow's feather I gave her when we got back, and the tattoo sheet still poking out from under her notebook. I smile at the irony, thinking that giving her a tattoo, even a fake one, maybe wasn't the best idea.

"Better sleep now," I say.

She turns on her phone, and in its glow I climb up into my loft. I make sure my magazines are stacked neatly in the corner, find Murphy, and snuggle in. I check my phone one last time before setting it at my feet.

In the last forty-five seconds, Ruth has liked every one of my Instagram pictures.

CHAPTER EIGHT

The next morning I'm already thinking about the Something Old part of my plan when I wake up. I glance at my phone, and Ruth's likes are still there. I smile and hop down from my loft, not even caring that my hair must look like I got dragged through a wheat field. "Morning!"

Ellie turns and smiles at me, a book in her lap. "Morning," she says.

I open the tiny cupboard above the sink and pull out one of those doll-size boxes of Trix you can get from a gas station. I set myself up at the table with a paper bowl and plastic spoon and pour my cereal. I'm thinking about how life in an RV with a bowl of cereal in your hands and a shipwreck ahead of you is just about perfect.

And then I look up and see Ruth.

She's leaning back with her hood up, eyes closed, and earbuds in. Her face is gray and I have to ponder for a moment, because she looks more virus-sick than anything else. Part of me hopes that's what it is, because if she's got something viral like a cold or a stomachache, that's something I can actually help her with.

If it's not that? If she's losing her appetite and having trouble sleeping because of The Pit? Well, that just doesn't seem fair. Maybe that's petty, but it's true. Aren't we on an epic trip to pirate ships? Wasn't talking with Ruth in the middle of the night the best time with her in a long time?

Her phone buzzes with what looks like a Twitter notification. When she opens her eyes and moves, a hint of color comes back into her cheeks and she doesn't look quite as nauseated. That *is* a relief, but then my own stomach starts churning with not knowing what to do.

"Hey, Ruth," I say, before she closes back up again. She looks at me, taking out her earbuds. "Are you excited or sad to leave New Orleans?"

Maybe there's a spark in there I can ignite.

Her eyes narrow. There's no spark.

"Want an orange or a yogurt or something?" I

say. Honestly, she looks like she needs to eat. I try to remember if this is how she looked when one of the failed medicines stopped working. Sometimes the wrong dose would make her sleepy or sleepless, or make her lose her appetite. One type even made her throw up, and I remember eating bananas and white-bread toast with her after she started feeling better. Is something like that happening here?

"I ate," Ruth says.

"You sure? I'll split an orange with you."

"I can't do perky this morning, okay, Olivia?" She leans back, puts her earbuds in, and closes her eyes.

Everybody gets tired, even Healthy Ruth. In fact, tired Healthy Ruth will sometimes come watch the National Geographic channel with me, bringing along a cup of her favorite pomegranate herbal tea. For Sick Ruth, though, even the tiniest interaction can be utterly exhausting. Sometimes, at first, it's hard to tell the difference.

"Ladies and gentleman," Eddie calls from the front. "Please keep your hands, arms, feet, and legs inside the vehicle at all times. If your destination is not Houston, Texas, you are on the wrong bus, but it's too late now!"

Eddie gives a whoop and shifts the RV out of park.

"You are so weird," Ellie says, grinning.

We back out of the lot and head for the freeway. For a while there is quiet driving. Ruth listens to her music, and I lie in my loft, clicking through my camera and listening to the thrum of Ellie and Eddie's conversation.

I take what feels like a million pictures of everything around us as we drive. I'm getting pretty good at maneuvering settings for motion shots. I even try to get some good pictures of my loft. I read a few articles from my *National Geographic* magazines.

Around one thirty we stop for lunch just outside of Baton Rouge. Eddie fills the RV up with gas and the rest of us head into the Subway next door. Maybe Ruth is distracted or hungry or tired, but for whatever reason she forgets to put her hood up, and when Ellie stands in line behind her, she sees the bass clef tattoo. The skin around it is still swollen and red, raised almost like a brand. That, I think more than anything, gives her away.

I see the moment when Ellie spots the tattoo. Her brow wrinkles, curious at first, before understanding waves across her face. She looks closely at Ruth, while Ruth is looking down at something on her phone. Ellie pauses for a few seconds, considering. A roiling starts in my stomach almost like I'm the one who's about to get in trouble. My mouth opens like a guppy out of water, but I'm not sure what to say or even who I'd say it to.

But Ellie's shoulders go up and down in a deep breath, and somehow I feel my lungs exhaling along with hers. I see tenderness and worry in the way Ellie looks at the swollen tattoo, like she wants to help, like she's worried about Ruth hurting. Ellie is here and knows what to do, and I'm not on the spot to smooth over a tempestuous situation. The fluttering in my gut eases up a bit.

That's when Ellie steps forward and puts a gentle hand on Ruth's arm. The soft touch doesn't jolt or jar Ruth, and she turns around to look at Ellie. So quietly I can barely hear what she's saying, Ellie says in Ruth's ear, "Let's step outside. I think we need to have a conversation."

Ruth stares at her, looking both guilty and confused. Ellie motions to the tattoo. Ruth's shoulders sink and her cheeks grow pink. Her mouth opens for a few moments, but she says nothing.

Ellie motions to Eddie through the window and as he comes in, she says, "Order for us, will you?" Then she and Ruth walk out the door.

Through the window I watch Ruth and Ellie. Ruth is looking down, arms folded, jaw clenched. Ellie is the one talking, and she has a hand on Ruth's shoulder. After a moment, Ellie puts her arm around her and pulls her into a side hug, but Ruth keeps her arms folded. After another minute they start walking toward the RV and Ruth pulls her cell out of her back pocket.

Eddie and I get to the front of the line. I remember Ruth's order, even the sauces, and Eddie knew Ellie's sandwich order without asking. We come out holding four plastic sandwich bags. Ellie is waiting by the front of the RV, and I catch the slight nod she gives Eddie, a *We're okay, I got this* kind of nod. As we get closer to the RV, I can hear Ruth on the other side, her voice an angry whisper.

"Because I'm old enough to make these decisions for myself, Mom," says Ruth. "It is so cliché that you are still treating me like a child."

A voice in my head responds, *It's so cliché that you're acting like one.* That voice scares me. I try to ignore it, keep it behind a locked door.

It's only another few seconds until Ruth comes around the corner and holds her phone out to Ellie. "She wants to talk to you."

My stomach plays one quick chord of wanting

to talk to Mom myself. Of wanting to hold the phone while Mom says she knows how hard this whole thing must have been for me.

That stomach knot comes from that same deep place in me, a place I try to keep the door shut on, a place where it would feel so utterly satisfying to put my head back and scream, *Everybody just shut up and be happy!*

We step up into the RV. Eddie starts the engine and we pull out of the gas station. I spread the sandwiches out on the table and start sorting them, but Ruth is huddled into her earbuds, so I eat alone.

Still, I watch my sister. Her face is carefully blank, and she's staring at her iPod, clicking the pen in her hand and jotting in her notebook. Again and again I wonder what she's thinking. Does she regret what she did? Or is it more a sense of righteous indignation? Is she annoyed by all the fuss and worry? Is she thinking about what other people think at all?

Up at the front Ellie speaks quietly into the phone, mostly *hmms* and *yeses* and *please don't worries.*

There are still four more hours until Houston. Four more hours until we reach my plan for Something Old, and I try to hold on to that thought.

Despite the tense lunch, and even though my Something New plan didn't go like I wanted, we're heading to a new city, and a new chance for the treasure shots.

At least the drive is pretty. The prettiest scenery we've been through so far. There are tall swampy trees on either side of us, so green they're almost glowing, sticking out of a muddy ravine. The perfect chance for about a thousand more pictures. Soon we're driving across an overpass as tall as some of the trees, concrete keeping us out of the swamp and marsh beneath. The sky is gray-blue.

A flock of egrets billows from underneath and flies deeper into the swamp. I take a dozen photos, but it's hard to get a great one when both you and the subject are moving so fast.

A couple hours later we pass over a bridge with a sign that says TEXAS STATE BORDER. It's got a picture of the Texas flag on it. I instinctively close my eyes and hold my breath as we pass the sign, making my same wish.

Ruth is listening to John Williams again.

Maybe the dinosaur skeletons at the Houston

Museum of Natural Science will lift her up, like the jazz concert did. On our original drive across the country, our Something Old day was at a museum in Fort Worth. We looked at fossils and dug up very old dinosaur bones. I took that picture of Ruth making a face like the giant T. rex. We listened to "Quest for Fire" by Iron Maiden and laughed at that picture for a long time.

"Whatever old things we don't like," Ruth had said that day, after we'd listened to all her songs, "they can just stay behind. Even things about ourselves."

I didn't know exactly what she meant then, and I'm still not exactly sure, but I *have* figured out where they have dinosaur bones in Houston. I've even asked Ellie about maybe going to the museum, and she said it sounds fun. Getting Ruth to do the same face is probably pushing it, but I could at least get a great shot of her looking up at a big old T. rex head or something like that.

My phone buzzes and Mom's picture pops up on the screen. I answer.

"Hey."

"Hey, sweetie." I like the way she says *sweetie*, like she's giving me a blanket and Malt-O-Meal when I'm home sick. Not condescending. "Everything okay?"

"Yeah."

"I'm sorry about what happened earlier. I know it's hard on you."

This is why it's so great talking to my mom. She always ends up saying exactly the right thing, and this time it's such a relief, all the words and feelings inside me crest like a wave and threaten to overflow. I want to tell her that it *is* hard. I want to tell her how stuck I feel sometimes, stuck in helplessness and not knowing what to do. But just this acknowledgment from Mom makes it easier for me to go back to being the person who lightens things. Tries to bring a little sun when things are murky. That's when I feel most like myself.

"It's really fine. I'm okay," I say.

"She's going to have some major compensating to do when she gets home."

I'm not sure what the sunshine response is to this. After a pause, Mom sighs. "Is she okay?"

I glance at Ruth. She's lying on her bed with her face to the wall. "I think so. Sort of."

Mom knows what I mean, and sighs again.

"We'll be there soon," she says, partly to reassure herself, I think.

"Totally," I say. "And Ellie and Eddie are here. Really, Mom, we're doing great."

I hear her turn on the tap. I imagine her in the kitchen, filling a pot to cook ravioli or broccoli or something. "You know," she says. "It's so much harder seeing you guys go through something difficult than going through it myself."

My throat catches. Mom's words feel like spotting my reflection in a mirror, or like she's defined something I hadn't quite known the words for until now. Even my bones feel like they're responding to how true this feels. How waiting and watching, being able to offer no tangible comfort, feels like being on a stationary bike trying to catch up to someone far ahead who's calling out for help. How I'd jump at the task of climbing Everest if only it meant bringing my family, bringing Ruth, some peace.

It's a relief to put such concrete words to my frustration. And, especially, to know someone else feels the exact same way.

I pull out my smiling voice. "That's why you're such an awesome mom."

"The force is strong with this one," she says.

"Guess what?" I say. "I was googling, and there's this museum, the Houston Museum of Natural Science, and supposedly it's got these awesome dinosaur skeletons. I asked Ellie if we can stop there."

After I hang up with Mom, I go back to my window. It's much greener than I expected for Texas, especially in the summer. There are tall trees everywhere, good for climbing. We pass several stucco apartment buildings. The sky is gray and threatening rain, and I hear the rumbling of thunder every once in a while.

There's a snort from below and I turn around. Ruth laughs, looking at her phone.

"I thought you'd get a kick out of that," Ellie says. She's turned around in her seat, looking back at Ruth.

"His mouth is so huge," Ruth says.

"What?" I say, peering over.

"It's a Steven Tyler meme," Ellie says.

Part of me wants to ask more, to put myself in on the joke, but I decide it's best to leave things as they are. Not only did Ellie manage to fairly seamlessly get Ruth on the phone with Mom about the tattoo, but she's gotten a laugh out of her afterward too.

I'm relieved.

And I wonder what Ellie has that I'm missing. Then my phone buzzes. It's a text from Ellie.

Ellie: *How's your arm?*
Me: *Much better, scrapes are going down.*
Ellie: *Any secret tattoos I need to know about?*

I snort.

Me: *Well I was thinking about getting something on my forehead . . .*
Ellie: *Ha. Ha. Not.*
Ellie: *In all seriousness, I know that must have been really tough and confusing for you. I'm glad you got to talk to your mom, and if you need someone in person to talk to, I'm just a spit take away.*

I look at my phone for a minute, not sure how to respond. I want her to know how relieved I am, that I want to curl up in my loft and let her and Eddie take care of everything. I also want to say something that will make her laugh, or at least make her worry a little lighter.

Finally I settle on something simple.

Me: *Thanks. I'm okay.*

Ellie: *Okay. If you're ever not, I'm here.*

We drive through downtown Houston fairly quickly. We start passing from tall business buildings to neighborhoods, and soon we pull the RV into the driveway of a small brown-brick home with a lawn so freshly mowed there are grass clippings lining the walkway.

A tall woman, her blonde hair up in a messy bun, runs out to meet us, and Ellie is the first one out of the RV. Darcy's got a tan that wasn't there last time I saw her.

I'm still in the RV and can't hear what they're saying, but Ellie pulls Darcy into a tight hug that lasts for a long time. I follow Ruth out of the RV. Finally, Ellie releases her daughter. Eddie puts his arm around her, and they all turn toward me and Ruth.

"Hey, guys," says Darcy. "It's been a while." She slides through her parents' arms and gives us hugs, first Ruth, then me. I've always thought her voice was deeper and older than her looks suggest. She looks Ruth up and down and grins, revealing two

112

slightly crooked incisors. "Cool hair," she says. "I could never pull that off." She sounds genuine, genuine enough that Ruth's mouth twitches up into a smile.

"Thanks," she says.

Ruth just ignored me last time I tried to compliment her hair. Two minutes with Darcy and she's already got a rare Ruth smile. I should be used to that bubbling of unfairness deep in my rib cage, but it still fizzes like tides against a cliffside every time. Of course, I don't say anything, though. I'm not going to make things worse.

"I had no idea this place was so nice," Ellie says. "And it's that cheap?"

Darcy nods. "Chelsea and I have our own laundry room and everything. And the basement has plenty of windows, so we get light. Come on, I'll give you the grand tour."

"You sure the Garcias don't mind the RV?" asks Ellie.

"No, no, not at all. They're super nice. And we have our own back entrance, so we won't be in their way at all."

The group migrates toward the side of the house.

"So what are college classes like?" Ruth asks, sounding like she's actually interested. "What are you studying again?" Like those moments with the meme, the tattoo, the plum, I've seen Ellie have some kind of magic that helps Ruth breathe just a tiny bit easier, and it's clear Darcy has some of that magic too.

Please, oh please, I think, *let it work wonders.*

And let just some of it rub off on me.

CHAPTER NINE

At the restaurant we go to for dinner, Ruth orders seafood like she usually does, although she barely picks at the shrimp salad and crab cakes. I offer her some of my barbecue ribs, but she says no and goes back to nibbling. I wonder if Ellie or Eddie notices in the midst of excited conversation with their daughter.

The happy news is Darcy keeps us all laughing. The three of them are good at telling family stories, the memories from their past, in a way that includes those of us who weren't there. Ellie tells us about a time when they all went to an art exhibit and spent over an hour looking for Darcy before they finally found her asleep under a bench in the Matisse room.

"We had called security and everything," she says.

"What can I say?" says Darcy, shrugging. "I was tired. Also six."

We're all laughing when the waiter comes to refill our drinks. Even Ruth manages a short snicker, and I'm glad. Maybe she's just been tired, or fighting off a summer cold or something like that. I'm still not exactly sure where the signs are pointing—normal blahs, virus, bad day, or something else. I'm still watching the signs.

And tonight, at this restaurant, I'm hopeful. It's sometimes a struggle for Sick Ruth to muster energy or interest in what's going on, even when it's something Healthy Ruth normally likes, so I'm taking her investment in the meal and the conversation as some good signs, and I relax a little.

I decide I like this restaurant a lot. The dark wood tables are classic, but the neon signs and posters crowding the walls and the chattering from all the tables around us add a casual, easy air. The sweet potato that comes with my ribs is overflowing with butter and cinnamon and marshmallow. The talking subsides, the sign of a good meal. It sort of fills you up all the way to your fingertips, and then you get into a rhythm.

Darcy is the first to break the silence. "So remind me what you guys are doing while you're here?"

"Oh yeah," Ellie says. "What was that museum you were asking about, Olivia?"

"Ooh!" Darcy interjects. "We should go to the aquarium! It's an absolutely awesome one."

"Aquarium?" Ruth says, picking apart a roll. "That sounds cool."

Ellie's looking at me and my brain starts clicking fast. If Ruth seems interested in something, that's important. Yes, the museum has dinosaur bones, like last time, but it doesn't have to be exactly the same, does it? All it needs is Ruth and Something Old. I could figure out something else, couldn't I? If Ruth wants to go to the aquarium?

"Yeah," I say. "The aquarium sounds great."

There's another thought in my head, telling me Something New already didn't go how I wanted, and now this, and don't I always end up compromising on what I really want? And then another thought. An even less happy thought. A question, wondering if Ruth would have thought the aquarium sounded cool if I'd been the one to suggest it.

Are these thoughts really me? What about the other thoughts, already beginning to flip through my mind, confident I can think of something great, even if it's not dinosaurs? Both voices are playing their song loudly in my mind, like earbuds playing a different song in each ear.

Darcy says something to Ruth, and Ruth laughs. Regardless of the confusing jumble in my head, there's a relief that comes anytime Ruth is happy. I home in on that and try my best to make my mental earbuds play that song the loudest.

We get a refill on rolls and honey-butter and keep eating and talking. Everybody is so relaxed— the warm rolls are probably helping—and for a while I feel that vigilant guardian in my brain relaxing too. We talk about our trip so far, about whether we're excited about school in the fall (me: yes; Ruth: meh). Darcy tells us about the summer internship she's doing, helping with an art class at the local juvenile detention center, and also the sculpture project she's working on.

"Oh, hey!" Darcy points at me. "My mom told me about your Instagram and I just kept staring at it all last night. I'm more a sculptor than a photographer, but seriously, you have such a different, unique eye for things. All your pictures are this almost strange, particular reminder of like, whoa, oh yeah, our weird world is kind of awesome."

I sit still in my chair, a little stunned. That may be the best thing anyone has ever said to me. She sees what I'm trying to do. What I desperately wish everyone saw.

"Thank you," I manage. "Wow."

As in my conversation with Mom, the perfect words have been given to me to express something in my mind that felt unclear before. On this trip, the support and enthusiasm from Ellie and Eddie has felt almost surprisingly wonderful, but this feels like Darcy's not only seeing and appreciating my pictures, but understanding them at the deepest level.

"I'm totally serious," she says.

"Me too," I say.

She smiles, then turns and says something to her mom. The dim lights and smell of barbecue float around me while my mind processes this, because Darcy has managed something kind of miraculous. Ruth is talking, watching things like they're important, like she's a little bit glad to be here. But there's something else too. In only a few words Darcy has made *me* feel important. Like she really gets me, and she's glad *I'm* here.

It all comes together in a very fragile and

alarming thought: She's made me feel how I'd want a sister to make me feel.

And I wonder if Ruth is thinking the same thing.

In the morning, I catch Ruth smiling while she puts on her makeup, and I see Dropkick Murphys playing on her iPod. Definitely a good sign. There's something fascinating about watching her put on mascara. One of my favorite parts of playing pirates with her when we were kids was spending over an hour in the bathroom while she gave me thick black eyes and bushy eyebrows and a sleek goatee. After Mom had bought us those face paints, of course. I roll to my side.

"Morning," I say. She clears her throat in acknowledgment. "Where is everyone?"

She sticks the mascara brush back in the tube and pulls out one earbud. "Ellie and Eddie went to see the campus with Darcy. They'll come pick us up later for the aquarium."

She's talking. Complete sentences. No snips of sarcasm. She's smiling. I need to thank Darcy one day.

I need to learn how to do whatever it is she did for Ruth.

My little pile of tattoo sheet and feather and concert program are still undisturbed on Ruth's shelf. I point to the program. "So is the concert your favorite part of this trip so far?"

"Probably," she says. "You? Camera still awesome as you hoped?"

"Oh yeah," I say, trying not to sound like I want to fling my arms around her waist for asking. "It's almost like the camera itself is better than my skill level, and I just hope I can get good enough for it."

"Well," she says. "What I know most about you is that you don't give up, so I'm sure you'll get there." She pops her brow liner back in her bag.

Where's pixie dust when you need it, because I've got everything else required to jump off this loft and float right up into the clouds.

Ruth tilts her ear toward the mirror and leans in. She's trying to get a close look at her new tattoo. The swelling has gone down a little bit, I can tell.

"What did Mom say about that?"

It comes out before I think about it too much.

Ruth looks over at me with an eyebrow raised,

a look somewhere between *who cares* and *none of your business*.

"Doesn't matter," she says.

I sit up and let my feet dangle over the ledge. "I mean, it kind of does."

Something new and daring is trilling in my sternum and pushing me on. So often I don't have the right words for things, and I'm not sure I do now, but in this moment I've got to try.

Ruth turns to me and folds her arms across her chest.

"I mean," I say, stumbling on. "It matters that you did something that made Mom worried. That hurt her." *And me*, I think. *It matters that you hurt me.*

Ruth takes a small step toward me. I'm tempted to pull my dangling legs up into the safety of my loft, but I stay still.

"Are you judging me?" Her words are quiet and dangerous as viper fangs.

"I . . ." Why am I doing this? It started out as such a perfect morning and now I'm ruining it. Now I've started, though, and I can't stop myself. This is something bigger than me and I *need* her to understand. "No, I'm not judging. I just . . . aren't there ways to . . . to do the things you want, to be yourself, without ignoring Mom and Dad? Without hurting them?"

Without leaving me behind?

Ruth boils me in another perfect pause before she takes two more steps forward. "You little prick," she says. "You have no freaking clue, Miss Self-Righteous. I'm sorry we can't all be as perfect as you. I'm sorry everything's not always rainbows and glitter, that some of us actually have hard crap to deal with in our lives."

"That's not—"

"Don't even." She jabs her finger at me like a cutlass. Now she's close enough I can see the intensity in her face, but it's not exactly what I expect. It's that hurt and suffering I've seen before, whirlpooling and storming and battling behind her eyes. "Congratulations on living in a world where you can control everything that's in your head, but don't you dare look down on me for at least having some say about what's *on* mine."

My throat feels like cardboard. My whole face is burning and my hands and my stomach feel shaky. All over my skin feels tingly and I wonder if this is how it feels to go into shock. I feel too panicked and scared to be angry. My mouth is closed like it's sewn shut.

In a movie, this is when somebody walks in, Ellie or Eddie or Mom, and there is a sweet but awkward scene where everybody talks things out and all the fights and problems are resolved. But not in real life. In real life, I stay frozen, staring between my feet that are still dangling off the ledge of my loft, until Ruth has decided she's won, decided that I have been sufficiently shut up.

I know in my head that this really isn't about me, that it's a battle between Healthy Ruth and Sick Ruth. I know there's that storm in her mind that I can't see. I know all these things, but still it doesn't change the freezing in my body, and I wonder, maybe, if that mental miscommunication is a tiny bit what she's dealing with all the time.

How can a morning change so drastically, like the sudden snapping in half of a ship's mast?

Ruth releases me from her glare, and I turn back to my pillow, barely mustering enough dignity to not pull my blanket over my head.

CHAPTER TEN

The nightmares started when I was seven. The story changed every night, but it always involved a horrible accident, someone in my family, and me— and it was always my fault. A car crash, a house fire. The part of me that knew I was dreaming would squirm and try to blink myself awake before the awful thing happened, but I never could.

One night the dream changed, just a little. This time the person with me was Ruth. She was hurt, bleeding badly. We were walking in a desert, part of a caravan of camels, and suddenly Ruth screamed and ran to me, her side oozing red. I had a special ointment, the only thing that could save her, in a pouch in my pocket. I'd found it by following a treasure map, and dug it up from deep in the sand. She screamed for me to help her, save her. She got close to me, showed me the hole in her side. I pushed her away. She screamed and I pushed her again. We kept walking, my camels and I, and Ruth stopped following us. I kept walking over the dunes while her screams and cries echoed across the sand behind me. I did not turn around.

I woke up from that dream with the front of my T-shirt drenched and cold with sweat. There was already a puddle of tears on the pillow and a sob was building in my chest that felt too huge and throbbing for my seven-year-old ribs.

When I could move, I slid out of my bed, my arms wrapped around me, and scrambled to my parents' bedroom. Mom had been sick all day and Dad was at a conference out of town, and when I opened the bedroom door, the bed was empty. There was a line of light under the door to the bathroom, and I heard noises of sick and smelled vomit.

I stopped, frozen with indecision. I desperately needed someone to hold me, to bring me back to the real world, but despite my terror I didn't want to add more to my mom's plate when she was already so sick. Even then I wanted to be the sunshine person. The person who made everyone else feel at peace, feel more happy. Storms always came, like sickness, but I wanted to be the person who made it all a little brighter, a little lighter.

So I stood still for a minute, then took two steps toward my bedroom. No, I couldn't—I was too scared. I took three steps toward the bathroom. Another retching noise, and I wanted to let loose the wail building inside me, but I didn't want to make too much sound or Mom would hear. I didn't know what to do.

"Olivia."

A whisper from the bedroom door. I turned and saw Ruth. Her hair was in braids, and she was still young enough to be wearing her pink narwhal nightgown. I must have woken her up.

"I . . ." Speaking felt too much like crying, and I stopped.

"Come on," she said, and motioned me to follow. I took in a couple breaths, trying to cool my burning face. I stepped toward her.

She put her arm around my shoulders and led me down the hall to her room. She opened the door and in the glow of the guitar-shaped nightlight, I stepped across her floor to the bed. She didn't say anything, just pulled back her blanket, and I climbed in, pressing my back against the wall. Ruth slid in next to me and pulled the blanket over both of us. She settled her head onto the pillow, facing me. She put an arm around me and closed her eyes.

Late in the afternoon, I finally become bored with my *National Geographic* magazines. It hasn't been the most eventful day of our trip, short of the morning's explosion. I've come down for food, but otherwise stayed bunkered in my loft. Ruth has been on her computer all day, earbuds in. Still listening to Dropkick Murphys, which is good. Maybe, I think, loud, rambunctious music is a weapon Healthy Ruth uses to fight that swirling, tidal wave battle in her brain. And that's much, much better than The Pit.

When Ellie, Eddie, and Darcy come back, they have a pizza for us. We load into Darcy's car and eat our dinner on the way to the aquarium. Ruth and I don't look at each other, but she and Darcy talk a little more about college and music. I listen to their conversation and feel somewhat calmer than this morning. I hope Ruth does too, and I'm glad right now she seems engaged.

As we drive, I look out the window for hypothetical pictures, watching the trees and redbrick churches, and by the time we stop, I'm smiling. I can't help it. In front of us is a gray building about three stories tall. There are balconies and rounded outcroppings, and it would look like a hotel except that the bottom story is designed and colored to look like red rock and sand. There's a fountain in the front and in the middle, two giant stone sword-fish, taller than me by far, leap into the air, the blue paint gleaming. Over the entrance are the words, AN UNDERWATER ENTERTAINMENT ADVENTURE.

I don't know exactly how my Something Old plan is going to work out, given that we're not exactly where I planned and Ruth is probably still uber-mad at me right now. But I'll do my best. I can't replicate the photo from before, but I'll still have a great Something Old picture to show Ruth when we get to the end of the Treasure Hunt.

I run over to the swordfish statue. I love how their bladed noses arch toward each other. I love the smell of the chlorinated water. I pull out my camera to take a picture. Not the best shot, but the light coming from the fountain looks pretty cool. I'll try for some really good shots once we're inside.

We walk through the sandy, cavernous entrance. A lady with tiny braids in her hair stands at the front counter and Eddie buys us tickets. The lights are dim and blue, making everything look sub-merged.

Past the lobby are three arched entrances, each bearing the sign of its respective exhibit. My eye is immediately drawn to the one on our right and my legs want to leap with the thrill of it. There's a sign made to look like sea-worn driftwood painted with red letters that say SHIPWRECK.

"Let's go there," I say.

I look back at the group. Ellie is smiling at me, and nods. Ruth is on her phone.

We head right, past some swampy-looking trees dripping with moss, and under the stone arch into a dark hall. There's only dim light, shimmering and blue, like waves. At the end of the tunnel is another arch, and through it I can see an aquarium wall and what may be, if my dancing heart isn't playing tricks on me, a giant sea turtle.

I step more quickly down the dark hall and through the entrance. We enter a room shaped like the hull of a ship. The walls above and below and all around are made mostly of thick glass, making everyone in the room a fully submerged participant in this underwater kingdom, this living Atlantis.

What I saw *is* a giant sea turtle. I crane my neck a little bit to see him past the rock he's hiding behind. A stingray as big as me swims so close I gasp and step back, but then step immediately forward again and watch the ray glide like a magic carpet over to a bed of algae. Fish are everywhere, some small and flashing colors any artist would be proud of, as well as giant sluggish things that look more like big rocks than fish, their faces in a perpetual scowl. Some of them look like they could swallow me whole, even if their size is distorted by the water.

Between my feet, the glass flooring reveals the underwater world and sandy floor below. Another huge ray sleeps in the sand, partially covered. Without taking my eyes away, I pull my camera from its case and focus in on the stingray. I bend down close to try to minimize distortion from smudges and glare from the glass. A spiky pink sea urchin by the ray's left eye completes the frame like it's a still life. I click. Another fish gets too close and the ray skitters up and away, leaving only a puff of sand behind him.

There's a short lady wearing round-framed glasses and an employee polo shirt standing by the entrance, and I step over to her when none of my group is watching.

"Hi," I say. "Can I ask you a question?"

"Sure," she says. "That's what I'm here for!"

"So," I say, "which is the oldest animal here? In the aquarium?"

She bites the inside of her cheek for a moment. "Hmm, good question." She looks around for a second until she spots what she's looking for. "That guy right there, I'm pretty sure."

I look where she's pointing and it's my good friend the sea turtle again. He moseys slowly along the glass, following some yellow fish.

"Awesome!" I say. "Does he have a name?"

"Oh yes," says the lady. "We call him Ned."

Camera in hand, I look for Ruth. She's looking down between her feet at a thick patch of pink coral. I keep one eye on her and one on Ned as he swims over our heads, and I try to triangulate myself between them to get a shot of both of them together, maybe even looking at each other. I try not to get too close so Ruth doesn't notice I'm kind of following her.

She groans, looking hard at her phone like it's just insulted her. Ellie notices too. "Everything okay?" she asks.

"It's nothing," says Ruth.

"You sure?" says Ellie.

Ruth glances at me, then looks back at Ellie. "It's nothing, just this songwriting contest I submitted to. I didn't win."

"Oh gosh, I'm sorry, Ruth," Ellie says. "That's got to be discouraging."

"It's whatever," says Ruth.

Ellie looks concerned, but lets it drop. I watch Ruth walk toward the glass, not seeing the stingray swimming right in front of her.

I take a couple of steps closer to her. Ellie, Eddie, and Darcy have meandered to other parts of the room. The shimmering reflection on the floor is like walking on light waves.

These are the kinds of Ruth situations I've always been terrible at, even before Ruth got sick. The knowing-what-to-say part. The comforting part. I can never get the tone right, like a singer always slightly off-key. I try, but can always tell I come off like a trite, ignorant cheer captain instead of someone who really cares. It seems like this should be such an obvious thing, comforting my sister. But somehow for me, knowing exactly what to say to make her feel better is like a bird knowing how to breathe underwater.

But I *have* to try.

Another step closer. I want her to know that I don't care about our dumb argument anymore, and I've put it behind me. That there will be more opportunities. That she should always keep working on her songs and her own things no matter what, because they're amazing.

Great. Even in my own head I'm a dumb cheerleader.

"Hey, um, I had no idea you were sending your songs to contests and stuff. That's really cool. You'll get the next one."

"Right," she says.

"Seriously."

"It's your fault, you know," she says, but her voice is soft, not mean. Like she's trying to joke. "Always talking about the job you're gonna have, the magazines you're gonna work for. Always reading *National Geographic*, practicing on Instagram and stuff. I have to keep up somehow, right?"

This surprises me a lot. Takes me off guard, even. *This* is what she's noticing? This is what she's seeing in my picture taking? I've been trying to communicate deeply with her—to reach her where she is—for so long, in so many different ways, and this feels sort of like she hasn't understood the words I've been saying, but instead has noticed something small I've been casually doing by myself in the background. Like I've been trying to show her these big, epic, meaningful landscapes, and instead she scrolls back to some tiny blurry selfie and says, *But what about that?*

I'm not quite sure what to make of it, but I'm happy for anything she's noticing. Anything that connects us.

"We'll both get there," I say. "We shall conquer!"

She looks at me and she looks softly sad.

"Maybe I'm just terrible," she says.

"Definitely not," I say. "The songs you've shown me are amazing."

"I don't know," she says.

"I do."

She sighs. "Thanks, but I don't know if I want to keep getting more of the same lame rejection without feeling like I'm getting anywhere."

I laugh. "'The Same Lame.' That should be your next song."

She doesn't laugh, but she doesn't roll her eyes either. "I don't know," she says again.

Ruth is talking to me, close to confiding, which, for me, is a kind of walking on light waves. But I worry her hands might be losing their grip on the edge of The Pit.

"I think your work is amazing, no matter what anyone else says," I say.

The same lame cheerleader words, but I'm not sure what else to say. I hope she knows I mean it.

"I appreciate your effort," Ruth says. "And I know it's all blue skies and happy sea otters in Olivia Land over there, but sometimes things just suck."

I see Ned out of the corner of my eye, but I keep focused on Ruth. "I know," I say.

Ruth clenches her hands and looks down. "I keep doing that to you. I don't mean to snap . . . it's not . . . I'm sorry. I'm really sorry about today." Ruth sighs. "Don't listen to me, okay? Be happy. Take lots of pictures."

I want to hug her, tight and long. So she knows I see the struggle, so she knows I know how creative and fun and thoughtful and loyal my sister Ruth truly is. I also want to tell her I'm trying to understand the best I can, and that things aren't always easy for me either. A voice in my mind says, happy otters can get hurt too, and then I'm remembering the way otters hold each other's hands and imagining what it must be like to be the person who takes care of the otters here at the aquarium, and all those thoughts make me want to grin, which

136

totally doesn't help my attempt to appear serious and understanding. Mature, like Ruth. Which, clearly, I'm not, or at least she doesn't think I am.

I don't say any of those things, though, because I've pushed enough for one day. Another blowup and I'd shrivel like a raisin, and besides, just being here with Ruth in the blue water lights, the way we've talked about things while silver fish bob around us . . . all of that turns this into a good day after all.

Ruth's turned back toward the glass and the water. I spot Ned the turtle again, coming from up high, toward Ruth. I lift my camera as fast as I can. He's almost in frame . . . Ruth's about to look up at him . . .

The room rings with a high-pitched squeal. I stop my instinct to turn around and instead I keep my camera lifted, fiercely trying to get this one shot, but Ruth's already walked away, out of frame.

I turn around and there's a little girl, maybe four or five years old, with perfect blonde whale-spout pigtails. She sobs in hiccups and plops down in the middle of the floor.

By the time I've realized she's probably lost her mom, Ruth is already kneeling at her side. I check around the room. Now that someone's taking care of the crying child, most everybody is going back to their own groups.

"You wanna know something?" Ruth is saying. I tune in to their conversation. "Guess how much percent I promise we'll find your mom and you'll be okay?"

The girl hiccups again, but the sobs have stopped. She's thinking hard about Ruth's question. "Nine?" she says.

"One *hundred*," says Ruth.

The girl's eyes get wide. And Ruth smiles.

I click a few photos. Something feels like it's happening here, so photos are my natural response.

"It's going to be one hundred okay?" says the girl.

"Yep," says Ruth. "And you know I'm right because I'm smart."

The girl considers again. She's practically chipper. "Yeah," she says. "And you have blue hair."

"That is absolutely right," says Ruth. "Let's find your mom, okay? Can you remember what color shirt she was wearing?"

"Abby!"

A woman with a baby in one arm and a spit-up stain down her left shoulder comes running toward us. She's got those exhaustion lines under her eyes and she practically melts onto the floor in front of the little girl.

"Honey, you have to stay holding on to the bag, remember?"

"I had to say bye-bye."

The woman sighs. "I know. Okay, let's go. Don't you want to see the octopus?" She stands up, a tight grip on her daughter's hand. She adjusts the diaper bag over her shoulder while trying to hold the baby in one arm and keep a handhold on Abby with the other. She pauses long enough to turn toward Ruth. "Thank you so much," she says. "Sorry, I'm all over the place . . ."

In the particular shrug of Ruth's shoulders, I can tell she has the exact right words for this situation, like an artist with custom paints.

"Naw," says Ruth. She looks back at Abby. "Hey, it's pretty sweet you have a mom who takes you to the aquarium, huh?"

Abby hops a little. "Yeah, to see the octopus like on TV."

The woman shakes her head and laughs. "She is weirdly obsessed with the Discovery Channel, I swear."

Ruth points her elbow over in my direction, but she doesn't look at me. "When she was little, my sister used to cry herself to sleep at night if my mom *wouldn't* let her watch *Shark Week*."

The woman laughs. Ruth smiles again.

"Anyway, thanks," the mom says.

"Have fun," Ruth says. Mom and daughter leave. As Ruth watches them go, her shoulders slump back down.

I have an imaginary conversation in my head, where I tell Ruth that things will be one hundred okay. What I *do* know one hundred percent is that in that hypothetical conversation, her response is an eye roll and a huff. And that's on a good day.

How come she gets to tell someone things will be okay, but I can't tell it to her? Just because she's sixteen and that girl was five doesn't make it any different.

And there's something else too. Ruth has had a pen cap between her teeth and a notepad on her lap for most of her life. She practices her words like Serena Williams practices serves. She's careful with them and uses them exactly the way she wants. So why do her softest ones seem to flow more freely to strangers than to me?

I try to hold tight to the good ones she just gave me, even if I wish I got them more often.

My hands, in their usual habit, hold tight to

140

my camera. We are here in the same place, Ruth and I, but if we each told our story of the aquarium, the two would be completely different, like we're experiencing this on opposite hemispheres. But isn't that what pictures are for? To show each other our stories?

Is it possible, even through the highest-quality lenses, for two people to really, truly see the same picture?

I have a couple of good shots of Ned the turtle, but none with Ruth in them. I keep clicking through my camera, scrolling past photos of sharks and turtles and the statues out front, up to the most recent ones. My stomach does that clutch thing when I hit the magic shot, the one that will be my post for the day. It's all silhouette. Ruth and the little girl, backlit in underwater blue. Ruth's shadow finger is pointing at a tiny trio of fish and the girl's silhouetted face is pointed up in awe.

"Just When I Needed You Most," Randy Van-Warmer, 1979.

CHAPTER ELEVEN

We have a long drive ahead of us. It's about seven hours between Houston and Fort Stockton, where we plan to stay for the night.

I tell myself it doesn't matter at all if Ruth is nicer to strangers sometimes. I mean, she was helping a little girl, right? That's a good thing.

Ruth looks very pale this morning. Paler than I've seen her in a while. I want to bring her soup and her old stuffed animal and the perfect songwriting gig, like Ruth sometimes talks about, all served with a magic kind of medicine that will make anything hurting feel better—one hundred okay—just like that.

Something Magic, like a Treasure Hunt? Maybe?

I really, really hope so.

Tomorrow when we get to Arizona it will be time for Something Magic. And as far as magic is concerned, it's good timing. I could use the extra help.

On the original trip, our Something Magic day landed on our stop in Little Rock, Arkansas. It started out as an awful day for me, because I'd lost Murphy somewhere the night before. I'd torn apart our hotel room looking for him. I looked under all the blankets, under the beds, in every drawer, even in the shower, and nothing. Ruth told me that because Murphy'd happened to go missing on Something Magic day, it meant he was off doing something magical, and that change was magic, even if it seemed hard at first. She told me it was all going to be okay, but even that didn't make me feel better.

We left the hotel for some brunch and a walk around. I was grumpy all through our meal, even though it was pancakes. We ended up at a bridge with tall metal spires and a metal grate along the side. As we walked across, the metal grate got more and more full of locks. Combination locks in all kinds of colors. Ruth told me they were wish locks, and that when you locked your wish in place, it would come true.

I guess my family is pretty amazing, because we went to a hardware store right away and bought one of those locks. They knew how much I needed that wish. Maybe I should have used my wish for something different, and maybe a ten-year-old is too old to be wishing for her stuffed killer whale to come back, but in that moment none of that mattered. I just wanted Murphy.

So I locked my wish in place, and took a picture of it for our Treasure Hunt, just in case. And guess what was waiting for me back at the hotel, resting neatly atop the newly made beds, like he'd never gone anywhere at all?

Something Magic.

There are no lock bridges in Tucson, Arizona, the city we'll be reaching tomorrow. (Plus, when I was researching, I found out putting locks on bridges can actually be pretty damaging.) But when I googled Tucson, I found something just as cool. A bridge, a highway overpass, covered in metal mesh in the shape of a gigantic rattlesnake, complete with a pointed, rattle-y tail on one end and gleaming red eyes on the other.

Definitely a bridge magical enough for a replica picture.

We say a long goodbye to Darcy before loading

into the RV. She and Ellie have made us all sand-wiches with turkey slices and avocado and Dijon mustard and honey-oat bread that totally look gour-met, even though I'm not usually a sandwich person.

I give Darcy a hug. "Hey, thanks for everything," I say. "I think your dad would say your superpower is making people feel relaxed. Easy with them-selves. I wish I could do that."

"Ha, that does sound like my dad," she says. "But hey, no fair if you took my power. Stick with your own, girl." She winks.

I try to remember what Eddie said mine was. Something about finding neat, pretty things to make people happy or excited. Ruth is in the door-way, tying her shoe. I just wish my power was to have whatever power people needed, to do exactly what they needed, exactly when they needed it, and I wonder if anyone has that power. It's almost a game, trying to think of powers in this way, instead of as specific things like flying or talking to animals or breathing underwater.

What would Ruth's power be?

"Have a fun rest of the trip," Darcy says, her arm still around me. "I'll be following your pictures. You're basically my family's official favorite pho-tographer."

"Ha, thanks."

I head into the RV, and Darcy begins her good-bye to Ruth. I watch from the window, wondering what they're saying. Maybe it's not possible to have the power to be everything for everyone every time. Maybe Darcy's right, and that wouldn't be fair. Or would it mean everyone was identical, with the same power? Would that be better or worse than one person's power not being enough?

Ellie is the last one to climb back aboard the RV. She gives Darcy a long hug first, delaying as long as possible the final drive away. When we've all finally said goodbye, we wave to Darcy through the window as we pull away. When we're officially on the road, I settle into my loft.

On our last trip, Ruth didn't really have a plan for our Something Magic days, because she said that's sort of the point; you can't plan for the magic. We found the *New* sign and the old dino-saur bones because we were looking for something specific, but Ruth said Magic is different. Magic you have to let happen, and capture it when it does.

Normally I'd agree with her, but since this trip is about repeating the pictures from before as much as possible, I *do* have a plan, even for Something Magic. An epic diamondback-rattlesnake bridge plan. And this time, I hope my plan actually works.

I go between checking my phone and watching the Texas sky swim past. The clouds seem like they're glittering, and I'm getting some really nice comments on my pictures. I think my pictures are even getting better. Good signs for Something Magic, I hope.

Out of the corner of my eye, I see Ruth sigh and turn up the volume on her iPod. She's wearing pajama pants and she looks like she might throw up. I'm still wondering if she's virus-type sick or if it's something else. If this is a wrong-dosage kind of nausea. The medication she's on has worked for a long time, but from the beginning Mom said things can change, and we'd take it one step at a time.

Ellie gets up from her seat and chooses a bag of chips and a Gatorade. Ruth's earbuds are in, and Ellie doesn't say anything to her, just opens the chip bag and sets it and the Gatorade at her side before sitting on the couch across from her. We both watch Ruth mindlessly reach her fingers into the bag and nibble on a chip or two. Again, just a few bites and sips of drink seem to help.

With all the Darcy activity going on, I had wondered if Ellie and Eddie were noticing any bad signs too. I'm glad I wasn't the only one. I'm glad they are here.

Ellie stands up to go back to the passenger seat and sees me watching. "Want some snacks?" she says, holding up her own open chip bag.

"I'm okay," I say.

Once Ellie's back in her seat, I lean over the ledge of my loft. Ellie looks up at me, smiling.

"Hey, I'm texting updates to your parents," she says, her thumbs hovering over her phone. I catch her glance over her shoulder at Ruth before looking back up at me. "Anything you want me to tell them?"

"Oh, just that I'm really glad you guys are letting me ride on the roof of the RV and I only fell off once."

Eddie and Ellie both laugh.

"Won't they be glad they sent you with us," Ellie says.

Ruth adjusts her earbuds. I try to remember some of the things Darcy said that made her smile.

"Ruth?" I say.

She clicks something on her iPod and raises an eyebrow in my direction.

"When we get home, what if you dyed my hair? Not like yours, but, like, purple maybe. Just the tips."

She takes the pen cap from between her teeth. "Mom would ground you and murder me," she says.

Why is it so easy for me to make other people laugh, but not her? Why is it so much easier for her to use her gentlest, most supportive words on strangers rather than on me? My hands ball into fists before I realize it. Ruth is back into her music. I just want her to listen. To hear all the things I'm trying to say. For one terrible moment I see myself ripping the iPod out of her hands and throwing it so hard at the window the glass shatters. The image scares me like a daytime nightmare. I think about pouring cool water on the steam inside me. I try, try, try to envision it evaporating away.

Texas is rockier than I expected. There are white chalky hills, jagged like cliffs, barricading our right side. We stop in a tiny town to fill up the RV with gas.

"Last stop for a while," says Eddie. "There's not

149

much between here and Fort Stockton, so if you need something, get it now." We all head into the gas station.

There are two hawks circling above our heads. I come out of the gas station with a blueberry muffin and chocolate milk and watch them. Birds usually fly away too fast for you to really see them, but these two stay right above us, hanging on the wind. They make me think of fire dancers, with the sun and us as the center of their circle.

Ruth is the first one back in the RV. I'm not sure if she's eaten anything but a couple chips from the bag Ellie handed her earlier, and she didn't get any food in the gas station. Her skin looks gray. While she climbs back into the RV, I stay outside to wait for Ellie or Eddie. I need to talk to one of them about this. To see if they're seeing what I'm seeing, or if things are okay and I'm overreacting. I wait and look at the sky and watch the two birds circle each other.

Ruth has gotten sick like this before, but the problem is that I don't know what it means. I don't know if it's a twenty-four-hour kind of sick or a back-to-before-the-medicine-started-working sick. She might just have some tummy bug. She might just need to sleep. But it might be much worse. She might be in the deepest, blackest kind of Pit. The kind that feels like a trap, like you're never going to be free of the dark again.

All I want is for her to be okay.

Ellie and Eddie come out together, holding hands and laughing. They look up to see what I'm watching.

"Those are some beautiful birds," says Eddie.

"Yeah," I say. "Hey, uh, can I talk to . . ."

"Ellie?"

We all turn together. A tall woman with dark but graying hair, tan skin, and gold hoop earrings stares at us. I don't think I've ever seen almost-gray hair look so beautiful before. She's standing next to a small green car with the gas nozzle in her hand. I'm glad she hasn't started filling up yet because from the look on her face she wouldn't have noticed if the nozzle started spurting out fire, let alone gasoline.

Ellie's usually vibrant face goes white, her mouth open like she's been punched in the gut. The look is so unusual for her, so unlike her happy exuberance, that I would be frightened except for the look on her husband's face—worried, but unafraid and full of tenderness. He puts an arm around her shoulders and strokes her arm.

I look down. I feel awkward, like I've walked in on someone naked. I don't want to be here, but I don't want to draw attention to myself by bolting to the RV either. I stand very still.

"Sofia Hernandez," Ellie says.

We all stand for a moment, staring silently, a triangle of pulling and pushing forces, like magnets. I look back and forth between this Ms. Hernandez and Ellie. The bell over the door dings. Still nobody moves. I catch a whiff of cigarette smoke.

Ms. Hernandez takes a step forward. Eddie puts a hand on his wife's back and sort of tilts her forward, and then the ice shatters and the two women fling their arms around each other, talking over each other, looking at each other, grinning, explaining, holding each other by the shoulders. The color in Ellie's cheeks is back.

"How . . . I can't believe this . . . how have you been?" asks Ellie. "What are you doing in the middle of Texas?"

"So, so good," says Ms. Hernandez. "I'm still working at the clinic, of course. I'm just on my way home from a conference in San Antonio. And you? How have you been? My, my, it's been so long. I haven't seen you since you were how old?"

"I wasn't quite eighteen the last time we saw each other. I can't believe you recognized me."

"Of course I recognized you."

"I'm Ellie Longmire now," she says. She turns and stretches an arm out toward Eddie, who comes to her. He puts an arm around her waist. "This is my husband, Eddie."

Ms. Hernandez shakes his hand. "So, so good to meet you."

"Likewise," Eddie says. "I've heard amazing things."

"It is so, so nice to see a happy story for one of my girls." Ms. Hernandez claps her fingers together like a prayer.

Ellie leans her head into her husband's shoulder, beaming. A big rig honks at us to get out of the way and we move over to the sidewalk. I move over with them and Ellie sees me.

"Oh!" she says. "And this is Olivia, basically our niece. We're driving to San Diego. There's Ruth too, in the RV."

"Wonderful!" says Ms. Hernandez.

"Olivia, this is Sofia Hernandez. She . . . she's a therapist. Mine when I was a teen. For a few years, actually."

"Dr. Hernandez?" I say, holding out my hand.

"I guess so." She smiles at me and shakes my hand hard. "Lovely to meet you, Olivia."

Ellie looks at her watch, then at her husband,

then at Dr. Hernandez. "It's only about four thirty, but do you . . . I think we have time for an early dinner. Would you want to grab some food and catch up for a bit?"

"That would be great!" says Dr. Hernandez. "I've got a few hours."

Eddie steps quickly up into the RV to tell Ruth, and Ellie and Dr. Hernandez keep chatting like best friends. Once I'm alone with Ellie I'll talk to her about Ruth, about what I'm noticing. Eddie steps back out of the RV again and puts a hand on his wife's shoulder. "Ruth's going to stay and nap," he says. "Not feeling too well."

Ellie's brow wrinkles. "One minute, let me talk to her."

She dashes up into the RV.

"It really is great to finally meet you," Eddie says.

"Glad Ellie found you," says Dr. Hernandez. "She's something special."

"She really is," Eddie says.

I watch the RV and wonder what Ellie is saying, and what Ruth is saying. When Ellie steps back outside, her forehead's still wrinkled with concern.

"She's . . . she's pretty set on staying," Ellie says. She points to a barbecue place just a little way down the street. "I told her we'd just go to that restaurant right there, and to text us if she needs anything. Does that sound okay?"

"Good plan," Eddie says. "And we'll bring back some food."

Ellie smiles softly at Dr. Hernandez. "I'd have loved for you to meet Ruth and talk to her. She's such a remarkable girl. I think you'd really like her."

"Ah," says Dr. Hernandez. "Another time, maybe."

"Maybe you can give me some advice," Ellie says.

In my head I vividly picture the easy afternoon this could be, Ruth smiling as she steps out of the RV to join us, all of us chatting and getting to know Ellie's friend, worry-free as we joke and lick barbecue sauce from our fingers. The picture is so clear in my mind that it seems unfair and unjust that the image can't develop into reality like film in a darkroom.

Eddie puts an arm around me. "At least you'll get to know one of the remarkables," he says.

"A true pleasure," says Dr. Hernandez.

Dr. Hernandez goes to move her car, and Ellie leans in toward Eddie.

"I'll keep talking to her," Ellie says, looking back toward the RV. "And I've been texting her mom too. If it goes any more downhill, I think we should stop at a doctor's office somewhere."

Eddie nods.

For a moment I wonder about asking the doctor we have right here already, but I guess it doesn't really work like that. Plus I'm still not sure if what Ruth needs right now is a Dr. Hernandez kind of doctor or something else. It's good to remind myself that Ellie and Eddie are here too, and can handle and take care of things. That it's not all on me.

And hey, Ellie running into someone so important from her past is pretty magical if you ask me. Maybe that's a good sign of what's to come.

We walk to the barbecue place a little ways from the gas station. It's so hot outside that by the time we make it to the restaurant, I feel sweat dripping down the front of my chest and pooling behind my knees. The heat is almost a tangible thing, its own entity. The road waves and ripples like the whites of a frying egg. All of us are sweaty and red-faced when we open the restaurant door, but thankfully we're greeted by a wash of chilled air. I can breathe again.

That's summer in Texas, I guess.

"I doubt the chefs here even need an oven," I say. "They can just step outside."

Everybody laughs. "You're a funny one," Dr. Hernandez says.

"Oh, believe me," Eddie says. "She keeps us all smiling."

It's amazing how much lighter those words make me feel and how quickly it lifts me up, making people laugh. So easy and natural for me to fall into normal cheery-Olivia mode. I think about Ruth not wanting to come with us to this restaurant and wish Eddie's words were true every time.

Most of the tables are empty, and there's one old man in a cowboy hat at the bar. A girl about Ruth's age, with earrings all up one ear, leads us to a booth at the front window. I watch cars driving by, people jogging and walking dogs, though I don't know how they're managing that in this heat, and listen to Ellie and Dr. Hernandez talk.

So Dr. Hernandez was Ellie's therapist when she was young. That means Ellie went to the same kind of doctor as Ruth. I know it's different for everybody, but I wonder if maybe that's why Ellie's good at talking to Ruth, reaching her without agitating her or being grating.

Our food is served and we dig in. It's nice to have a cool drink. Maybe I don't know exactly what happened with them in the past, but I do know that Dr. Hernandez has the tiniest hint of an accent and is fun to listen to. Her eyes get wide when she speaks and her eyebrows raise like she's telling a vitally important story, even if it's only about the time she got asked out by her AAA mechanic.

Ellie turns to Eddie. "Will you text Ruth and make sure she's okay?"

"Already did," Eddie says, holding his phone out. "She says she's fine, just resting."

I've already texted Ruth too. Texted her a picture of the dancing cartoon hamburger on the menu. She didn't respond to my text.

"How . . ." Ellie starts. "How do you deal with it every day? That's got to be impossibly hard."

There's a sudden tension in the air between us, like guitar strings pulled tight. We're all still, even Dr. Hernandez. Only Eddie seems to know what to do, and he slides in close to his wife and puts an arm around her waist.

"Yes," Dr. Hernandez says. "It is hard, especially when things don't end as well as this."

The guitar strings between us vibrate, like they're playing a song. Ellie nods several times, her lips pressed tight. Her eyes glisten. Eddie strokes her hair.

"I remember one time," Ellie says, "you told

me nobody else could control or be in charge of my happiness or unhappiness. Whether they were right or wrong, fair or unfair. I still have something like that written up on a card on our bathroom mirror."

"She does," Eddie says.

I don't really hear what they say next because those words spin around my mind like a hamster running on a wheel. Nobody can be in charge of someone else's happiness. But what does that really mean? If that was true, was it pointless to try to help? What did that mean about hunting for treasure? And Ellie had just said that it was Dr. Hernandez who'd helped her, hadn't she? So was that Dr. Hernandez charging up Ellie's happiness or not?

Dr. Hernandez reaches across the table and puts a hand on Ellie's wrist. "It's good to see you again, Ellie."

CHAPTER TWELVE

There is something primordial about driving at night. I can lie down in my loft and press my head against the front window so I have the most complete view of the night sky. The sun has been set for a little while now, and we'll be pulling into Fort Stockton a couple of hours later than planned. But that's okay.

It's worth it to have a while for driving under the stars. And out here in this middle-of-nowhere stretch of Texas, the stars are thick enough to be a quilt.

It's different, too, driving versus being still. I've spent basically every night on this trip looking out this window at night while everyone sleeps, even in the bigger cities where the stars aren't as visible. But this time, with the world passing by beneath me, I feel more a part of the road and the stars and the night.

The green has largely gone away, replaced by more rocky cliffs and little tumbleweed shrubs. The treelessness is fascinating to me. It's like the universe put all the trees in one place and all the stars in another.

There was a tiny used bookstore by the barbecue place and Dr. Hernandez bought me a book about "Black Sam" Bellamy. I picked out a book for Ruth too. A John Lennon biography. When we got back from dinner, I gave Ruth the book and Ellie gave her the take-home order of barbecue shrimp, and we both kept an eye on her until she'd eaten a bite or two. She even read a bit of the book.

Ruth's sleeping now. I feel better when Ruth is sleeping. Sleeping is restorative. Sleeping is a good sign.

Even though we're behind schedule, and I'm trying as hard as I can to be patient about getting to the pirate ships and our treasure box, a dinner break and a free book seem like pretty good excuses for a delay.

I hear shuffling and whispering below me. The sound of a map being folded. I turn over and Ellie's head pops up to the ledge of my loft.

"Can I join you?" she asks. "I better check out the loft at some point, right?"

We both grin, and I scoot myself over to one side to make room. Soon we're both lying on our backs, looking through the window at the stars while the road continues to pass below us.

"Now this is cool," she says.

"Right?" I smooth my blanket and it's like my loft is a house I'm proudly displaying.

We're silent for a while. My eyelids are finally starting to droop. The light from passing cars washes across the roof like a tide.

"It was cool to meet your friend today," I say. "If you get a chance, tell her thanks again for the book."

"I'll tell her," Ellie says. I glance over at her. Her eyes are shut. There's something in her voice, a quiver.

"So she was your therapist?" I say. Then I quickly add, "Not that you have to talk to me about it, if you don't want."

Ellie smiles and tucks a gray strand of hair behind her ears. She doesn't speak for a few seconds, but then says, "She's a child psychologist. A therapist with social services. She helps kids when hard things happen to them. Some of those kids are dealing with horrific—I don't know how she does it."

I nod, even though her eyes are closed. I don't want to say anything and risk breaking the flow, risk reminding her who she's actually talking to. How young I am.

She helps kids when hard things happen to them. How old did Ellie say she'd been the last time they spoke? I've known Ellie my whole life, so sometimes I forget I don't know that much about her childhood, about her life before she married into our family.

"For me it wasn't . . . nobody hurt me physically, and I'm grateful for that." She opens her eyes now and looks at me, her face half-hidden in shadow. "I've told you before, I grew up mostly with my grandma, right? I was just a bit older than you when my . . . my mom left me there. I . . . I didn't handle it well. I kept having these . . . these thoughts about just disappearing. Disappearing from myself. My poor grandma was too old to be raising a teenager anyway, but she knew enough to find me someone to talk to. I really needed help when I went and saw Sofia."

The radio, barely audible, changes from a toothpaste commercial to a classical piano piece. We lie there, letting ourselves be enveloped in the notes and the whoosh of passing cars. I feel my insides shattering a little, imagining what Ellie went through. Again that sense of unfairness rises from my stomach. Nobody should have to go through anything like that, especially not someone like Ellie, someone as warm as the baked foods she gets excited about, who always seems to know what the people around her need, even if it's just a road trip game or a bag of chips. More than anyone, Ellie deserves that rainbow-cotton-candy world Ruth is always teasing me about. Nobody hurting her. I scoot closer to her and she puts her arm around me and I lay my head on her shoulder.

This is when words are not enough. *You are very brave*, I want to say. *I am so sorry. I don't know how anyone could hurt you.* But the words don't come close to what I really mean.

"I . . . wasn't sleeping for a long time. I felt . . . I wasn't sleeping, but I just felt so tired of everything. I just wanted everything to be quiet and leave me alone, and at the same time, I didn't want to feel alone. But it wasn't even as . . . as clear as that. I wanted to be sad, but I couldn't. I wanted to be angry, but I was just too . . . too worn down. Sometimes I would start getting ready and would just look in the mirror and think, what's the point. Sofia told me that my brain was living in that space between a dull reality and this . . . glittering, shining perfection I expected life to be. Felt betrayed when it wasn't the bright, golden light I had envisioned. It took me years to figure that one out. How to spot the little tiny gems and jewels of life again. Sofia was an important part of that. She's why Darcy's middle name is Sofia."

Bright, golden light.

Something glittering, shining.

The thing that's been lurking under the waves of my mind all day breaks to the surface: those first moments pulling into our new home years ago. How for me it was the treasure at the end of an adventure: Something Gold. I think Ruth thought it would be gold for her too. For the first several days we explored together, excited. We unpacked our things. We got into the routine of a new place, a new city. Now I'm looking back and remembering how the initial enthusiasm faded from the way Ruth talked, the way she walked around the house, the way we played. She started wandering through the house quietly, searching, like she was looking for something that wasn't there, like she'd woken up somewhere she didn't expect to be. And how maybe I'd been too caught up to really notice.

And then later, those memories from before Ruth got a therapist and medicine to help her. Those days and weeks and months beforehand, watching Ruth stumble around the house while the shell around her got thicker and thicker like a crustacean, and how maybe she was thinking about disappearing too. Her constant tiredness. How the music she listened to in her room got quieter and quieter until it stopped. Was she sad? I would ask. She would say no. And that was true; it wasn't really sadness. It was an absence. No real feeling, not like contentment, but like a vacuum. No music, no pictures. No pirate stories or anything remotely like treasure. Nothing, nothing, nothing; no Somethings at all.

That is the real Pit.

And without really wanting too, I'm thinking about our kitchen in Tennessee, and coming down the stairs toward it, and that bottom step that creaks. The spaghetti pot unwashed from the night before, that night in those worst weeks. Coming down past my bedtime, my feet in seahorse socks, for some late-night orange juice, and hearing Mom and Dad at the table. Hearing squeaking chairs on tiles. Hearing Ruth's name and the urgent pressure in my mom's lowered voice. Hearing my mom say,

I am so scared. What if things get worse? What if they get worse and worse until . . .

Her voice trailed off. That *worse and worse until* lingered in the air and in my ears with no answer to follow. I wanted my mom to say something else, to finish her words with something happy. I wanted my dad to answer that everything was going to be all right, that there was a solution out there somewhere. But neither of them spoke, and that *worse and worse until* echoed in my skull. Worse and worse until what? I never wanted to find out.

That night I walked quietly back upstairs, skipping the squeaking step and skipping the orange juice.

Ruth's therapy visits started soon after that.

If I'm honest, I think those words have set up home deep under the ocean of my consciousness ever since. Ever since, I've known I needed to do whatever I could for my sister; to turn my volume down if things were too loud for her.

I try not to be too happy now.

It's quiet in the RV, except for the rumbling of the road. For a long time, Ellie and I stay together, close and silent. Ellie's eyes are closed again. My brain literally can't imagine looking around and seeing only pointlessness. There are always too many exciting things possible in a day for it to be pointless. I want to know what to say, how to respond, but I don't.

Ruth would know what to say, I think.

Ruth would understand.

Sometime in the middle of the night I wake up. I blink a few times until I realize there's blue light coming from somewhere below me.

Ruth's awake too, and on her phone.

Silently as possible, I climb down from my loft. When I sit on the side of her nook, there's a creaking sound, and she jumps.

"Oh geez, Olivia, you scared me," she says. Then she gives a smile. A very tired smile.

I want so badly to give her that meaningful something from my conversation with Ellie, but that something is deeper than words, and I don't know how.

"Sorry," I say. "Couldn't sleep?"

"What else is new," she says.

In the light from her phone, I look again at her shelf. The tattoo, the feather, the program, now a ticket stub from the aquarium.

"Hey, maybe we could add all that stuff to a new treasure box or something when we get to California," I say. I think again about how, somehow, it's easier to ask important questions and say important things in the middle of the night.

The screen reflects in her eyes. "Maybe," she says. "I'm still . . ."

She hesitates. I wonder how much of my face she can see in the dark. I decide to prompt her forward. "Still . . . ?"

"I'm still looking," she says.

"Still looking?"

"Yeah. I . . . I used to like things."

Maybe it's the hope of the treasure we're heading toward; maybe it's being around Darcy or talking with Ellie; or maybe I'm just getting a little older, but for the first time, I think I understand what she really means.

"You're looking for something that's like it used to be," I say.

She makes a sound that's not quite a hiccup. She doesn't say anything in response, and I sit there for a moment until I realize my hand's on her foot.

Her voice is soggy with effort when she says, "The feather is really pretty."

CHAPTER THIRTEEN

The sky swirls gray when I wake up in the morning. No rain yet, but before I've been awake for five minutes, I see multiple flashes of lightning far off. Thunder woke me, I realize. For a while I just lie there, watching the gray clouds come in.

It's Something Magic day.

We are on the winding-down days of our trip, or at least the driving part. We have an eight-hour drive to Tucson today, and I text the information for the rattlesnake bridge to Ellie and Eddie.

I lean over the edge of my loft. "Hey, I just texted you guys the link for this rattlesnake bridge in Tucson that I found. Do you think we'll have time to stop there?"

"Rattlesnake bridge?" Eddie says, keeping his eyes on the road. "That sounds cool!"

Ellie checks the link I sent her. "Maybe we can stop there before we check into the hotel," she says. She glances out the windshield and up at the sky. "Unless the bridge gets hit by lightning before then."

Get Ellie and Eddie on board with my Something Magic plan: check. This time things will work. Then tomorrow we'll drive the last six hours from Tucson to San Diego. San Diego and Sunset Cliffs, where Ruth and I will dig up our Something Gold, our final treasure.

Plus scuba tours start the day after that. I'm so electric with excitement that I feel like I'm going to be a target for that lightning. I want to pull my camera to me and cuddle it. I can see the underwater picture in my head, the glow of light above the water rippling through the waves to the moss-covered wood of a ship.

I grin to myself and stretch. Maybe it's the increasing nearness of Wreck Alley, maybe it's waking up to a thunderstorm, but my veins are buzzing.

Ruth is slouched against her pillow, her hood pulled low enough I can barely see her eyes from this angle. I send a thought her way, hoping maybe she'll catch it and look up and smile, but she doesn't. The white cords of her earbuds stream from the hood like IVs. Finally she does see me, and when she catches me looking, she turns onto her side, facing the wall.

We go out for pancakes. Ruth comes to the restaurant with us, but I only see her stab at her food without taking any bites, and mostly she sits there looking like she wishes she hadn't come. I pour a cup of orange juice and slide it to her.

"Want to try some of my sausage?" Ellie asks.

Ruth shakes her head.

After breakfast Ruth is the first one to climb back into the RV. Ellie steps to the side and takes out her phone, and I stall long enough to hear her.

"Hey, me again," she says into the phone. It's the voice she uses when she's talking to my mom. "Yeah, she doesn't seem to be doing much better . . . No, no, don't cancel your conference lecture yet, but I'll text you the website for this clinic in Tucson that Eddie found."

I climb back up into the RV.

Doctors are a good plan. And my plan—my plan is a good one too. It hasn't really gone like I wanted, that's true, but maybe from now on it will, and if we can just make it to the treasure, make it to Something Gold, maybe it will be the kind of glittering treasure to lighten wherever the dark corners are in Ruth's mind.

Now Ruth's back on her bed and I'm in my loft and we've finally left Fort Stockton. The rain has started. It's coming in a steady sheet over the windshield.

My mind is too buzzed and drizzly to focus on reading or taking good pictures. I've been attempting to read for almost an hour, but now I lay the book open on my stomach and put my hands under my head. I let my mind wander for a while. It goes to the normal things—treasure, pirates, pictures. Ruth.

Maybe all these things are bubbling around in my brain like ingredients in a cauldron, coming together into a perfect Something Magic picture.

Today would be a really good day to find some magic somethings, that's for sure.

My legs are jittery. I lie on my back, my knees bouncing off each other until I feel bruised.

The rain is still pounding, making plinking noises on the roof.

We've been driving for hours. I check on Ruth again. She's sitting up in bed, earbuds in, a pencil hovering over the notepad in her lap. I see metered lines, scribbles on the page corners.

She's writing a song. Her face has a little more color. Maybe she did eat a few bites of pancake? Maybe they're starting to do some good? The page is not quite half full.

I climb down from my loft, going to the fridge as an excuse. Maybe she'll still be up to talking with me, like last night.

"Working on a song?" I say. I do my best to keep my voice casual, nonchalant. The surest way to shut her up is to make a big deal out of it.

She nods. I get a plastic spoon and a yogurt and sit at her feet. She doesn't roll her eyes or tell me to move. The eraser of her pencil rests between her lips and there's a crease along her forehead. Her eyes are still pained and dark, and this close I can see beads of perspiration along her hairline. There's something frantic about her scribbling and erasing.

I want to ask her about Something Magic, but instead I say, "How much does it cost a pirate to get her ears pierced?"

She lets her pencil drop to her lap and looks at me. "Huh?"

"A buccaneer," I say, and my straight face collapses into a grin.

She gives me a little shove with her foot and now she's the one trying not to smile. "Weirdo."

Ruth puts the pencil tip between her lips again and goes back to glaring at her notebook.

"What's your song?" I ask. I'm risking overstaying my welcome, and I'll leave her alone soon, but I want to take every chance I can get. Her eyes are wide and there are odd blotches of color on her cheeks. I'd be more worried, but she's sitting up and talking. I don't know what to think.

"I need a word," she says.

"Starboard."

Roll of the eyes, but more friendly this time. "No, I mean like . . . um, I don't know. Something about like, how unpredictable life is? Or not quite that. Like, that it's bigger or different than we think it is? And love is like that too? I don't know, that doesn't make sense."

I think of my favorite vocabulary word from English class. It'd make a good Treasure Hunt word one day. *"Chimerical."*

She looks up at me. She's biting her pencil now. She pauses for a moment, and I can practically see the word making its way across her forehead.

"That means, like, whimsical, right? Or like, unreal?"

"Yeah. 'Unrealistic and wildly fanciful.'"

She hovers her eraser over the page. "Then if I changed *you* to *all* . . ." She erases a few words, writes in something new, adds another sentence at the end. Her lips mouth the words as she reads through it.

She looks up at me, and the smile on her face is wild, searching, sad.

"Thanks," she says.

The Christmas I was six, Ruth and I each got a stuffed animal in our stocking. I got Murphy. His black-and-white face and beady eyes peeked out over the white fur trim of my stocking. I scooped him up first thing. That year I hardly noticed any of my other presents.

Ruth got a stuffed penguin with a slightly crooked left wing. She named it Yoko. (She was going through a Beatles phase. At age nine.) She also got a DVD with all the Beatles TV specials and Mom made popcorn and we watched them all. Ruth focused on the DVD and tried to act like she was a little too old for stuffed animals, but she brought the penguin to watch the movie with us and slept with it that night. I remember hearing her talk to someone and when I opened the door, she looked embarrassed and tossed Yoko to the foot of her bed. "Knock!" she yelled.

A few weeks later I stayed home from school with a cold. Mom was sick too. The movie I was watching ended and Mom was sleeping, and I didn't want to wake her up.

So I pulled Murphy off my bed and took him on an adventure around the living room couches until I decided he was lonely and needed a friend. I opened the door to Ruth's room and took Yoko off her bed.

I took the killer whale and the penguin back to the living room and played Treasure Hunt. I wasn't so good at coming up with the words myself, so I used *singing*, a word Ruth had used for one of our recent Treasure Hunts. I played that they were in a band together, a killer-whale-and-penguin duo. I took them all over the house, looking for all the Bluetooth speakers. I took them to the piano, to Mom's round brush that looked like a microphone, to the mantel in the living room that was the perfect stage. I played until I was too tired to think of any more singing treasure. I took Murphy back to my room and collapsed on my bed for a nap.

I left Ruth's stuffed animal in the living room, and Ramses, our dog, got to it. Guess he couldn't control himself when he saw the perfect chew toy lying unattended in the living room. When Ruth got home from school, her penguin was ripped and shredded across the whole main floor, headless, gutless, every limb torn off except the misaligned left wing. And it was my fault.

Dad took Ruth to the mall that night and let her pick out whatever animal she wanted, plus a Ringo Starr poster. Ruth came back with a pink elephant that she never slept with, put the poster above her bed, and didn't talk to me for a week. We didn't play Treasure Hunt for even longer.

CHAPTER FOURTEEN

An announcer on the radio interrupts a foot cream commercial to give a monsoon warning. He says we're beginning the wet season for the southwestern United States. Which, at the moment, is us.

We passed through El Paso about half an hour ago, and there are still four more hours until Tucson, but Eddie and Ellie are giving each other worried looks. The rain is coming down so hard that the highest setting on the windshield wipers can hardly keep up with it.

The water is haunting. Hypnotizing. *Magic*, even. I sit with my nose inches from the window, looking at the world through a sheet of rain thicker than the glass.

The trees and leaves, though sparse, are whipping

and flapping like those inflatable tube people in front of car dealerships. There are fewer and fewer cars on the road ahead of us, which has turned into a black lake.

"I don't know," Ellie says below me. "I'm getting nervous."

"Yeah, me too. How close is the next town?" Eddie asks.

I peer over the edge, watching them upside down. Ellie pulls out the atlas. She runs her finger along the thick black line she sharpied in before we left.

"Las Cruces," she says. She opens the map app on her phone to double-check. "Twelve miles. Can we make it that far?"

For the next ten miles, it feels as if the motor home itself is holding its breath. I climb down to the couch and watch the rain through the side window and trade anxious glances with Ellie. Eddie seems intently focused and, thankfully, calm, although I have a feeling it's a very willful calm that will only last until we're safely parked and he can stop driving. Ruth has her earbuds in and is watching the rain too, but she doesn't exactly seem scared. She's watching the storm like it annoys her.

A tree branch flies across the road in front of us, missing our windshield by just a couple feet. Ellie gasps so loud it's almost a scream.

"How much longer?" says Eddie. His teeth are clenched now.

The wipers are hardly keeping up with the deluge at all anymore, and we're down to under twenty-five miles an hour. The radio announcer keeps making his monsoon announcement, telling everyone on the road to be careful, and telling everyone else to stay inside. Towns are beginning to lose power. We pass a line of cop cars and a rolled minivan on our left.

We finally see the Las Cruces exit. Eddie pulls off the freeway and the street goes down through a ravine so filled with water I have doubts about whether the RV can cross it, but we do, and then Eddie points us uphill. I see a flock of crows diving into the swaying branches of a desert willow.

"Where should we stop?" Ellie asks.

"I don't know," says Eddie. Both of their voices are just a bit loud, as if the storm is inside the RV, and they have to shout to hear each other.

We pass a gas station and a four-story stucco Holiday Inn. We pass several auto shops. Everything is so flat and treeless, except for a tall and jagged range of mountains to our right. And now it is all filling with water like a swimming pool.

There's a Walmart up ahead with a huge parking lot. "Let's stop there," Ellie says. "We need to get off the road."

Eddie nods. Just a few more yards. We turn into the Walmart parking lot and Eddie stops the RV. As he shifts into park and shuts off the engine, the pounding and swishing sound of the rain gets louder. For a full minute we all wait in silence, listening to the raging outside.

There are tumbleweeds flinging themselves all across the parking lot. Tumbleweeds are the strangest thing to me, like nature wanted to create herself a toy. Every time a bush lands on the ground, a splash of rain follows it on its bounce.

Now that we're off the freeway, we can all breathe a little easier, and maybe even enjoy the crackling storm.

After a moment Ellie looks back at me. "I'm not sure we're going to make that snake bridge tonight, Olivia. I'm sorry. We'll see if we can make it tomorrow."

"It's okay," I say.

And it really is okay, because I've realized something. We've landed in Las Cruces, the first place where we stopped on our original cross-country trip, the place where Ruth and I did our Something New Treasure Hunt and found those murals. So maybe this is a sign. Maybe this town and this storm are leading me to another Something Magic, even if it's not the bridge. I look through the sheet of rain washing across the window and wonder if maybe our Something Magic, this time, will be a stormy pirate battle between Anne Bonny and Mary Read and the infamous Davy Jones himself.

"You guys okay?" Ellie asks. "Anybody hungry?"

"Did we get batteries for those flashlights?" asks Eddie.

While they're talking, I've climbed back up into my loft, and lean over the edge in time to see them glance at each other.

Ellie looks outside at the ground between us and the store.

"We need food and batteries," she says.

The two of them stand and move toward the door. "Okay," says Eddie. "We're going to make a run for it. We'll be back in a bit."

As soon as they open the door, the rain and the crashing sound of wind sprays into the RV. They hurry out but have a hard time shutting the door. Finally they get it shut and we watch them splash their way into the store. The setting sun is obscured by swirling black clouds. The sky really does look like it's sparking with magic.

A flare of lightning illuminates the mountains, now straight ahead of us. They look more jagged every time I see them, jagged enough to make me think of sharks' teeth. That's what they should be called, the Shark Tooth Mountains. I'll have to look up their real name sometime.

I turn over onto my stomach, my chin resting in my palms, feet kicking like a metronome. It's such a perfect storm.

"Hey, Ruth," I say. "Know any ghost stories?"

"Nope," she says.

Back to her earbuds and paper.

"Ooh, do you think I should text Ellie about water? We should get water bottles. Running out of water would be bad."

Ruth mumbles something.

"What?"

"Go outside, open your mouth, and look up."

Something like that storm outside shivers down my back. This close to the windshield, it's almost like being on a pirate ship in the middle of a tempest. Easy enough to pretend anyway, or get the feeling. And I'm with a version of the Ruth who talked with me last night and told me important things, and then let me help her write a song this morning. Kind of. I'm going to get that Ruth back. I *have* to, now, in this storm.

"That thunder is crazy, huh?" I say, flipping my legs over the edge of my loft.

Ruth is hunched into her earbuds.

Just look up at me, won't you? I think.

No. This isn't going to happen. My sister is going to be here with me, enjoying where we are, enjoying it with me, us together in the middle of this pirate ship storm.

"Ruth," I say.

In that gesture she's perfected, that motion I've started seeing in my sleep, she pulls out an earbud and rolls her eyes. "What now, Olivia?"

"Wouldn't it be freaking awesome if there was a storm like this above us when we were diving?"

"You know that's not how it works."

"But it would still be awesome," I say.

She rolls her eyes again.

"What's wrong?" I say.

She raises an eyebrow like I've asked the stupidest question in the world. Like I've asked Benjamin Franklin if his kite experiment was a little shocking.

"Maybe I don't even want to dive pirate ships.

Just go back to flipping out about rain to yourself, okay?"

It's like Ruth's taken a magazine of all our games, our Anne Bonny and Mary Read, our couch-cushion planks and bedsheet sails and all our Treasure Hunts, and slapped me across the face with it.

"Not dive pirate ships?" I say.

"Honestly, sometimes it's like trying to sleep with a flashlight shining in your eyes."

"Not dive pirate ships?"

"It's like living with canaries that won't shut up."

The storm whips and rages behind me. Instead of shriveling me up, her words steam under my skin, but I focus on the crucial point.

"What about our box?"

Now she looks up at me, and though her voice is quiet, her eyes stab. "That's the other thing," she says. "I've been playing along, but how can you be so freaking naive? You think that stupid box is still there? Look outside, Olivia. Look at the real world for a change. You think that box would survive *this*? And this is one day, let alone years and years. Are you kidding me? Right now, that dumb cave is completely submerged, and that stupid box has been swept away and lost—"

My arms push me off the ledge before I think

about it. It's a fairly long drop from the loft to the floor, and my knees vibrate with the force of landing. But I don't fall. I will *not* let my plan fail, and that thought propels me forward like a wave. I step toward my sister. Her eyes widen enough for me to know my leap surprised her.

"I want you to tell me we're going to find that box," I say. "And then I want you to come outside with me and take pictures in the rain."

She gathers herself and picks up her iPod, slides it into her pocket and starts lifting the earbuds to her ears. "Can I be left with some semblance of normalcy and privacy for two seconds, please?" she says.

It's like the wind and crashing thunder have started storming inside my skull, and I yank the earbuds from her hands, ready to tug them away, but Ruth snatches them back.

"What the—"

"Why? Why?" I ask, backhanding the air.

"Calm d—"

"We're in the middle of a monsoon in the desert. With people who are taking us to pirate ships and probably buying us chocolate right now. Look at that storm. Can't you see it's magic? *Magic?* That box . . . we put that box there, all those things. I mean, don't you remember? Don't you remember the Treasure Hunts? We'll go to the cave again, together, and it has to be there, it . . . or something. Something is there. Don't you understand? How can you not get how . . . how important that is?"

Ruth's mouth opens, but I barrel on like a tsunami with miles of wind building up behind it. My whole being is laser focused and I understand in this moment how storms have eyes, how those eyes see nothing but what they're pointed toward.

"And not once, not *once* have you let me be excited. About the treasure box, about the ships. One time. And you know what? You think I don't get it. You think I don't get that things are hard for you. I mean, you say that often enough. I'm some stupid, idiot puppy to you. Well, you know what? It's not all peaches and roses over here. You have no idea because it's all about you; you don't care about anyone else's problems. You don't listen. Can you really not think about someone else for *two seconds*?"

Ruth's eyes are wide, wide, wide, and there's an ocean inside them, and she stares at me while our currents whirlpool and our tides clash.

"Ever thought about having a sister who won't talk to you? Who treats you like she wishes you weren't there? Ever thought about that? Know how many phone calls with Mom on this trip have ended with talking about how I'm doing? Zero. Like, zero. It's *how's Ruth*. Always. Think about how many times she goes to bed without worrying. None. You do realize that, don't you? And it's sure as heck not because of me."

I can't shut up.

"Do you have any idea what I've been trying to do this trip? For you? Every time I've tried to . . . but when someone else talks to you, if I said it, then it wouldn't . . . why can't you do just this one thing for me? Just once? Why do you not see . . . why doesn't this storm matter to you, or the ships? Why doesn't our box? Our Treasure Hunts? All our Treasure Hunts?"

It's like I'm speaking past the years and years caught in my throat. We haven't stepped into the rain, but my face is wet.

"Why don't I matter?"

And there it is.

All of it. Everything I've been holding in, bursting from me as raucous and tumultuous as the rain bursting from the clouds.

The air hangs between us like a minor chord. Like a camera shutter left open.

I let my words and my hurt bore into Ruth. I will not look away.

But her gaze isn't fighting me back. Her eyes are unfocused. Her forehead looks clammy and there's a strand of hair sweat-stuck to her left temple.

Her throat clutches.

And then her pupils flip back under her eyelids.

And she slips, slips, slips down to the edge of her pillow.

CHAPTER FIFTEEN

My fault.

We're in the hospital waiting room.

I've got my camera bag clutched to me. Not intentionally. It was a survival mechanism, an instinctual response, to grab it and hold it tight on our drive to the hospital.

When it happened, I called Ellie and Eddie. I could barely talk. Eddie called an ambulance. Ellie rode in the ambulance with Ruth. Eddie and I followed in the RV, Eddie silently white-knuckling the steering wheel, the shock and roar inside me louder than any storm.

Now the three of us are in the waiting room: Eddie, Ellie, and I.

Ellie says Ruth is starting to wake back up.

Ruth was moaning. Now we're waiting for the doctors to tell us what's wrong. To tell us how bad it really is.

And it's all my fault.

I did something to set it off. I let out my meanest thoughts, the monsters in the darkest caverns of me. I let them all loose and it broke everything. If Ruth never wakes up again, then the last thing she'll have heard is me yelling at her. Me acting like pirate ships and treasure boxes are more important than her.

This isn't what I meant. This isn't what I wanted. The words I said didn't mean what she thought they meant. Pirate ships aren't more important. Digging up treasure was just supposed to help things. To fix things.

After what feels like days and days, we're all brought into a gray room where Ruth is lying on a bed. We're told she's not unconscious now, just sleeping. We're told to be quiet.

Why couldn't I have been quiet?

She's okay, the nurse tells us.

Severe dehydration, the nurse tells us. Lack of nutrients. Ruth wasn't eating or drinking or probably sleeping enough. We tried. I thought we were trying, trying hard, trying everything, but it wasn't enough, and it still caught up to her. It caught up to all of us.

Ruth will be okay, the nurse says. Ruth has tubes coming out of her arm that are pumping her full of fluids and good things. She will be okay.

But I know the truth.

I know this is my fault.

Not eating or drinking are obvious bad signs— signs of The Pit—and what I tried didn't help, couldn't help. I should have seen how serious it was. I should have done *more*.

Mom and Dad are driving to the airport right now. The next flight to Las Cruces leaves at 2:01 in the morning and they'll be on it.

Ruth will have to stay in the hospital for a couple days. When my parents get here, they will coordinate a doctor to come and talk to Ruth and maybe change the medicine she takes so it might be better at helping.

I need to be better at helping.

We all sit in the gray room for a long time. People walk past our door and nurses poke their heads in every once in a while and check on us and check the monitors that Ruth is hooked up to. I've seen her eyes flutter a couple of times. She hasn't woken up, but her breathing is normal.

Then a curly-haired nurse in pink scrubs walks in. "Ruth had these in her pockets," she says. "You're her sister, right?"

She's looking at me and everybody else looks at me too. I nod, and the curly-haired nurse hands me a Ziploc bag. Inside is a tube of ChapStick, earbuds, and an iPod.

I can't sit in the gray room anymore. When the nurse leaves, I tell everyone I'm going to the bathroom. I have Ruth's iPod and earbuds in my pocket, but nobody asks about them.

I walk down the hall, past the restroom, through the lobby, and out the front doors. The rain is still coming down in torrents. We've been washed ashore here in this sterile place, bruised and scarred.

The storm feels better than it looks, washing down my face and back and arms. My hair will be plastered to my head, but I don't care.

Ruth's iPod is in my hand, my body its attempted shield against the rain. I realize I don't remember the last time I held or looked at it. No reason to, I suppose. But it's been a long time. Years, even. The storm pounds down on me and I put in the earbuds, ready for the music and the rain to rock me. I scroll down to her playlists, ready to shuffle through.

The playlist names—I recognize all of them: "Something Purple." "Something Singing." "Something Imaginary." "Something Flying."

"Something New."

"Something Old."

"Something Magic."

"Something Gold."

These playlists are all of those things—everything. From what I can tell, these are the last playlists she was listening to, the same playlists we'd listened to together years ago. Maybe this is what she's been listening to this whole time. I wish it was possible to take a *National Geographic*–worthy picture of titles on an iPod screen.

Aerosmith. Queen. Mötley Crüe. I let the wind and the loud music whip me around like a shredded sail.

When I realize I can't feel my toes, I turn back around and go inside. Ellie is there, watching me through the glass door. I'm worried she'll say something about me dripping water all over the hospital floor, but she says nothing, only wraps a white towel around my shoulders, uses another to pat down my hair, puts her arm around me, and leads me back to Ruth's room.

Ruth's still asleep. I still have her iPod in my hand, and I towel off any leftover raindrops.

"I know everyone's starving," Ellie says. "If I go find some food, is that okay? Eddie went to get pajamas and toothbrushes from the RV."

"Yeah, that's fine."

"You'll be all right?" Ellie says.

"I'll be all right. I'll stay with her."

Ellie nods, then walks out the door.

I take the empty seat by the bed. The lamp on the nightstand highlights half of Ruth's face. Her eyebrows are very highly arched. I never noticed that before. And her chin is so small. Where did she get such a petite chin? We look nothing alike.

She shifts, moans. Her eyelids flicker open. Her eyelashes look short with most of the mascara rubbed off.

"Hey," I say.

She closes her eyes, groans, and clutches at her stomach.

"Oh, hey, here." I grab the vomit tub from the table and lay it on her lap. She holds it to her chin for a few minutes, dry heaving, but nothing comes.

196

A few strands of saliva web her lips. Finally, she lies back into her pillow.

"Water?" I ask.

She shakes her head. Her eyes are closed. After a few minutes, I wonder if she's fallen asleep again.

"Why are you all wet?" she asks.

I take her iPod out of my pocket and set it on her lap. "I was listening to this outside. I . . . I really like your playlists."

Somehow I know she's not going to be mad.

I pick the iPod back up and put it in her hand, and for a second we're both holding it. The purple under her eyes is the color of survival. For a second we both have our hands on the earbuds.

She smiles, then she looks sad. Her throat bobs. "I was gonna make a new playlist. For this trip. But I . . ."

Her hands tighten around the hospital blanket. She doesn't finish her sentence. She doesn't have to.

Ruth is here. All of her, all of her happy and sad music, good and bad signs. And all of me is here too.

I will keep hoping for good things. Magic and gold things. I will pray for strong rigging.

"I wanna show you something," I say.

My camera bag is on the counter, above the cupboards with tongue depressors and more plastic throw-up tubs and all the other patient-room supplies. I slide my camera from the bag and when I head back toward the bed, Ruth scoots over and pats a tired hand on the blanket. I sit next to her.

I click through the display screen until I find the picture I'm looking for. I angle it toward Ruth.

"Your hands holding the concert program," I say.

Her eyelids blink slowly, but she says, "Hey, that's cool. I like the stage curtains in the background."

I point to the bottom corner of the program, to tiny letters that say *New Orleans*.

"Something New," I say.

Ruth's mouth opens, but she doesn't speak.

I click through to the picture of Ned the sea turtle. Again I show Ruth. "Something Old."

She stares at the picture. She taps a finger on Ned's green nose.

"That rattlesnake bridge I was asking Ellie about?" I say. "That was going to be Something Magic. And for Something Gold, a picture of the two of us holding our treasure box."

Ruth's hand rests on the camera.

"You did the . . . This is why you wanted to take pictures at that graffiti so bad," she says.

I nod.

"Sorry," she says. "I'm so sorry."

I think of all the things I said to her tonight. "I'm sorry too," I say.

They aren't the perfect words, maybe for either of us. No words will mean exactly what I want them to, but for now, these will do. I reach over and find her hand and hold it and she holds my hand back.

We stay like that for a while.

Then she says, "Show me the rest."

I turn to her and give her my best full-on, wide, emoji-worthy, puppy-dog grin. "Okay!"

She laughs.

I slide the camera back up toward us, click on the display screen, and we start from the beginning. I show her the shoe picture from Café du Monde. We look at pictures of the graveyard, pictures of trees on the side of the road whipping past, and the high-angle shot I took of Ruth in her bed. We linger on the silhouetted picture of Ruth and the little girl at the aquarium.

When we get through all the pictures, Ruth leans back in the bed and closes her eyes. "So,

Miss Travel Photographer," she says, "where are we headed to next?"

"Either New Zealand, for the diving, or London, when you and the internationally renowned band you write for go on your grand European tour."

"Eight-week tour, minimum," she says.

"I'll take pictures of you and the band on Abbey Road."

She rolls her eyes the friendly way. "Duh, of course. If . . ." She pauses, looks down at our hands, then back at me, then back at our hands. I think she's trying to find the right words for something. Finally she just sticks out her tongue in faux annoyance and says, "If you don't bug me too much before then."

Maybe it's the rain, maybe it's her music, or maybe I'm just getting better at it, but this time I think I know what she's trying to say:

If I'm up for traveling. For anything. For leaving the house. It's unknown and uncertain waters, sis. That's what she's saying.

Here's what I've learned about The Pit. You don't really have a choice about falling into it. You just do.

Maybe one day we'll go to New Zealand or London.

Maybe we'll watch *Edward Scissorhands* and *The Twilight Zone* for three weeks.

I'll be there, either way. Holding on to the rigging.

"I'm sorry," Ruth says again. "I'm sorry you were worried."

"Psh," I say. "Don't even. We worry about each other. That's what sisters are for. Besides." I squeeze her hand. "You also make me happy. You like your weird little sister's pictures on Instagram and send her funny selfies and appreciate the random things I bring you, like bird feathers. I mean, you know better than anyone that sometimes I'm helpful and sometimes . . . not, and sometimes I probably push things too hard, trying to make them exactly what I . . . But anyway, the point is . . . the point is, my life wouldn't have treasure hunts without you."

She gives a laugh that's very close to crying. "Not so much on this trip. I haven't been my . . . I've been having a hard time and you get the worst of that."

"Heck," I say, "I'm the one who just, like, volcanoed at you."

She gives me her wide-eyed look, but she's grinning. "You did, didn't you? That was . . .

unexpected. Honestly kind of impressive. I didn't know you had it in you."

"Oof, I didn't either," I say, guilt splashed across my face. "And, Ruth?" I pull her close until I'm holding her forearm tight against me, carefully letting the IV cords flow out from between us. "You never, ever, ever, need to apologize for being sick."

I think of the whole pile of things we've done together, been together, and while we sit on the bed, I feel the truth of those words settling in me like an anchor on the ocean floor.

"Olivia?" Ruth says. Her throat bobs again. "You *do* matter, you know."

"I know. I'm sorry for what I said. I—"

"No, listen. You're my . . . my no-filter person." She sniffs and wipes a strand of plastered hair from her forehead. "My free person."

It takes a moment, but her words breeze in and fill me, like oxygen filling empty lungs. At least in this moment, the constant, anxious buzzing at the back of my mind is still.

I say, "Because I'm your barnacle little sister and you know you're stuck with me for life no matter how much I bug you."

She leans back into the bed and sighs like her whole body is exhaling. "Something like that, yeah," she says. The grin she gives me is exhausted but utterly real.

It's strange how normal it feels talking to Ruth right now. Like some wide, deep river was between us before and we tried shouting across to each other but couldn't really hear. And now we're in the middle of the river, both of us.

I watch her lying there, her eyes closed, and I think, *If humans weren't so drownable, we'd never have invented sailing ships and submarines.*

"Actually, I changed my mind," Ruth says. "I could use some water."

I fill a plastic cup at the tap and hand it to her before sitting in the bedside chair. She takes a sip, gives another exhale, and gives the cup to me.

"Thanks," she says.

I hold her cup in both hands and lean back in the chair. "Anytime."

CHAPTER SIXTEEN

My favorite picture from the trip is one some-one else took. Ellie took it the night we were at the hospital. In the picture, my arms are draped across Ruth's legs. We each have an earbud in one ear. We must have fallen asleep listening to Pink Floyd or Philip Glass. The light from the lamp illuminates half of each of our faces. Running between the fingers of my right hand is a tube from Ruth's IV.

I called it *Treasure Hunters*.

Mom and Dad spent a good long time talking with Ruth in the hospital. And then in the hotel where we rested and slept and watched *The Twilight Zone* for a few days. Ruth took long, restful naps, ate spoonfuls of peanut butter and handfuls of popcorn while we watched TV, and even had a couple phone calls with her therapist.

Ellie and Eddie went between checking in on us, driving around southern California in the RV, and sneaking extra time at the beach. Ellie said that when we get home, we'll have a party with lots of treats and I can put on a slideshow of my best pictures. I showed them the picture I took of Ned the sea turtle, and every time they came to visit at the hotel, they brought me a new sea turtle figurine or key chain or necklace. I'm super excited about the new turtle collection that will definitely take the spot on the top of my dresser once we get home.

During our hotel R&R days, Mom bought these big one-hundred-milliliter water bottles and boxes of Crystal Light mix and Dad ordered up a big platter of shrimp cocktail, Ruth's favorite. She ate half the platter all on her own and Mom watched her and was smiling at her the whole time.

I also got to order up French toast from room service. *My* favorite. In the middle of our *Twilight Zone* marathon, we rented *Babe*, and Ruth even smiled at the singing mice.

That first night in the hospital, when Mom and Dad arrived just before the sun was about to wake up, they talked to the nurse and the doctor and

Ruth and made sure she was okay. Then they both wrapped me in a hug sandwich and asked me if *I* was okay. I knew if I ever needed anything, if I ever wasn't okay, they would keep me wrapped up like that until I felt better. Right then, though, I hugged them back and told them yes, I was okay. It was the truth.

And now we're all diving pirate ships.

We went to the beach a week after the hospital. After a week of sleep and food and water. After my parents had conversations with the doctors and Ruth's therapist, making sure this trip, this dive, was still going to be all right. At the beach, all the adults sat with the towels and treats while Ruth and I walked along the sand to our cave. We both walked slowly.

"You okay?" Ruth said.

My face must have been putting on quite the anxious show considering she was the one asking that question.

"Yeah," I said. "Yeah. I'm glad we're finally here."

"Me too," she said.

Then we were at the cave. We stepped inside. The space still felt huge. There were boulders big enough for climbing piled up in the middle, just like before, and a big circle in the ceiling opening up to the sky. This place had always seemed like a cathedral to me.

We didn't immediately walk over to the far corner where we'd buried our box. Instead, I ran my hands along the yellow rock walls. Ruth followed behind me, until slowly I touched my way into the shadows.

Both of us remembered right where to dig. We hadn't brought shovels, but dug in wrist deep into the sand. We sped up our digging, flinging sand like dog-paddlers. We dug until the shadows shifted. We dug until our hole was a foot wider and two feet deeper than we both knew it needed to be. I flung one last plum-size rock out of the empty hole and sat back against the cave wall. Then Ruth sat back too, next to me. We didn't say anything, just felt our sand-raw fingertips and listened to the seagulls caterwauling above us.

"Well," Ruth said finally. "I know it's not what you hoped. I'm sorry."

The tide slept low outside the cave, but inside my own skin it rose and rose and rose. A tide of all the things I couldn't change and couldn't control. Good days, bad days. Sisters, music in other people's ears, thoughts in their brain. Treasure buried in the sand. Even photographs, like the photographic subjects themselves, could shock me. Take me off guard. Could be full of surprises. New, old, magic, gold surprises.

The tide spilled; not a storm, but a release. And Ruth knew just how to scoot over closer and how to put her arm around my shoulders. Just how, after a moment of letting tears streak down the dirt on my face, to gently lift both my feet and set them into our hole, next to her own feet, and then push sand over them again and again until I managed to sniff myself together and start shoving sand in too. Until both our feet and legs were buried calf-deep. Until I started laughing, laughing from that fresh, deep part of me, until Ruth caught it too and we laid our heads back in the sand and looked up at the hole to the sky and laughed wildly until even the seagulls were outdone.

We can't control the waves and the tides.

But we can swim in them.

I am breathing underwater. It's been over a week since the night at the hospital. We are floating around coral and sunken ships with thick goggles and flippers, and oxygen tanks on our backs. It always surprises me how light the burden of those tanks is when you're submerged.

My camera is doing well in its special case. Ruth and I swim around the stern side of the ship. The professional divers, our guides, keep an eye on things from above us. Mom, Dad, Ellie, and Eddie are all around here somewhere too, looking at fish and sea turtles. Eddie's biggest goal is to see an octopus.

The water is tinted a misty green. There's rough, scaly coral plastered over almost every surface, and little tubes and ropy things and pricklys sticking up out of the sand. There are pops of yellow and purple through the green water, and starfish clinging to the sides of the ships. Peering in through rusted-out holes and broken beams makes me feel like a true Treasure Hunter, a true explorer. We swim in and out of the remains of the ships like squeezing in and out of rib cages. Bits of seaweed hula all around us like they're listening to a song.

With just the pictures I've got in front of me right this moment, I've got more than enough for a lifetime. More than enough to keep going.

I snap picture after picture of Ruth running her hands along the hull, swimming down face-to-face with the coral.

Ruth takes a turn with the camera too. A clown fish darts like a bullet from his anemone, right in front of my goggles, and scares me so bad I nearly lose my oxygen. I'm pretty sure Ruth caught the moment on camera because even through her goggles and breathing mask I think, right now, she's laughing.

Another picture for the "Sisters" folder. There's a lot to add.

People, I think, are not so much like oceans or puddles or rivers. I think they're more like planets, whole planets, with all kinds of oceans and puddles and rivers of their own. Some people splash easy, some people dive deep fast, but we're all sinking and swimming together.

I dive to the ocean floor and dig my fingers into the sand. I swim around the ship's side and put my nose inches from the old, mossy wood. The world here is green. Every snapped beam, every crooked mast, is a story. Multicolored fish swim in and out of the cracks and gaps and holes.

A hand on my shoulder pulls me from my glazed-over daydreaming. It's Ruth, of course. She taps her head, like she's had an idea. I nod. She puts her hands in circles and holds them up to her goggles, looking through them like binoculars. I must look confused, because she holds her hands out, thinks for a second, then starts signing. The letters come slowly to her hands; it's been a long time.

She signs: T-R-E-A-S-U-R-E.

Treasure. Treasure Hunt.

I nod again, this time so hard I nearly bang my head on my tank. If it were possible to bounce underwater, I would be.

We give each other the okay sign. Then I shrug to say, *What's our word?* She gets it, and pauses to think. She signs again:

B-R-E-A-T-H-I-N-G.

Breathing. Our Treasure Hunt word today is *breathing.* I wish I could take a picture of the entire planet. O-K-A-Y, I sign.

Something Breathing.

Maybe I'll find rocks that look like lungs. Maybe I'll take a picture of the way waves go in and out like a sigh. Maybe I'll manage a close-up of a fish's gills.

Something Breathing.

I watch Ruth swim away, looking for treasure. As Ruth swims, she glides into a sunbeam from the surface. It catches her and she looks up, her flippers sashaying below her. Bubbles from her mask pop on their way upward.

I lift my camera.

I take a picture.

ACKNOWLEDGMENTS

For all my treasures—

SOMETHING NEW
When I wrote the earliest drafts of this story back
in 2013, it's probably a good thing I didn't know
how much digging and exploring and soul-
searching and revising were ahead of me. I've re-
written this story so many times I've lost count, but
what I do know is that at each step, I've had people
helping and supporting me, and each of those
people has added something new and helped me
bring this story bit by bit closer to its true form.

To Kim, Jessica, Jen, Bridey, Tiffany, and Room-
mate. Thank you for being there from the beginning of this story, when Johnson was still a thing.
Thank you for helping me learn, mature, and grow
in empathy, and for forgiving me and putting up
with me when that learning and growth was slow.
I couldn't have written this without you.

Thank you to Ellie Terry, Cindy Baldwin, and
Amanda Rawson Hill for taking a chance on this

story in Pitch Wars '16. Dear reader, if these women and their books are new to you, get thee to a bookstore, because their books are treasures indeed. Thank you to all my Pitch Wars friends for supporting and believing in me when I was well and truly new.

Thank you to Ellie and Madeleine for your invaluable sensitivity reads and wisdom about mental health representation. You are both incredible, and any errors are mine.

To John Bennion, Dawan Coombs, Chris Crowe, Martine Leavitt, and the other amazing English department faculty at BYU. Thank you for letting me write a children's novel for my graduate thesis, and for the encouragement and supportive environment you fostered. I hope you know how precious that was to me.

To my new #roaring20sdebut friends. You've already helped me more than you know.

SOMETHING OLD

My oldest treasure, my parents. Thank you, Mom, for bringing me to the library whenever I wanted, for reading to me, and for having the most passionate and empathetic view of people and the world of anyone I know. Thank you, Dad, for your endless wisdom and passing on your book addiction. When I was little, you said you thought we were friends before we were born. I think you were right.

Oh, my siblings. I love you so much, and I could not have written this without you. Thank you for always supporting me in my crazy schemes and dreams. If I die first, I'll save our spot for the heavenly Fantasmic!, right in the back center by that trash can. I've got the blankets. Bring funnel cake.

Thank you to my grandparents. You four are like the corners of a tent protecting me against a storm. Thank you for providing such a solid foundation. Thank you to all my aunts and uncles and cousins, and I know there are a lot of you (a *lot*), but I hope you know how much I've learned from watching you over the years and how much each of you means to me.

SOMETHING MAGIC

With all the carving and chiseling and adding of new things with each draft, ultimately I needed someone truly magical who could fix all the unwieldiness and bring this story to life. That person was Melissa Warten, editor extraordinaire and true magician. I had such high hopes for this story from the beginning, and you've absolutely taken it above and beyond. If this story is whole, if it breathes, it's because of your sparkling wizardry. Thank you, thank you, and to the entire FSG team for making this story happen.

(And thanks to my magic feather. You know who you are.)

Thank you, also, to Brianne Johnson, Allie Levick, and the other fabulous magicians at Writers House. You brought this story to its perfect home and have always had my back. I would be stumbling through a magicless desert without you.

A wide-eyed, awestruck thank you to cover artist Alisa Coburn for somehow taking these two characters I've had in my head for so long and putting them so perfectly and magically in color. You are nothing less than an art alchemist.

SOMETHING GOLD

Which brings me to you, dear reader. You are my gold at the end of this Treasure Hunt. You might feel most like Ruth, or you might feel like Olivia. Either way, you are worth more than all the gold in the universe. The maker of this universe filled it mind-bogglingly full of treasures of all kinds, everywhere you look, and He treasures you, you specifically and individually, above it all. I do, too.